TO CRAIG:

EXIT OUT
OF THIS ADVEN[...]

Timothy Bartlett

July 30/2017

# THE GAME MASTER TRILOGY

## Book 1 - The Games People Play

*ENJOY THE BATTLE OF WITZ!*

*Timothy R. Bartlett*

TIMOTHY R. BARTLETT

authorHOUSE®

*AuthorHouse™ LLC*
*1663 Liberty Drive*
*Bloomington, IN 47403*
*www.authorhouse.com*
*Phone: 1-800-839-8640*

*Published by AuthorHouse 3/5/2014*

*ISBN: 978-1-4918-7067-9 (sc)*
*ISBN: 978-1-4918-7066-2 (e)*

*Library of Congress Control Number: 2014904372*

# CONTENTS

# DISCLAIMER

Each of the characters portrayed in this fictitious novel are purely co-incidental and are _**not representative**_ of anyone, individually or as a group of people, alive or deceased. They are the creation of this writer's imagination and used to produce the fabricated settings and events for the reader's enjoyment.

Try _**not**_ to take anything in this novel personally! _**None**_ of the storyline corresponds to any real events. This is a work of complete fiction and meant only for entertainment purposes (_while a person's grey cells get an active workout_).

Are you ready and willing to take on this challenge?

Then let us begin…

# WARNING

Some disturbing settings and bad language, in this novel, are used. This author apologizes ahead of time for any offence this may cause some of his readers and hopes the reader understands it in the context of the drama - as it unfolds.

## *I would like to dedicate this novel to the following*:

To my former roommate: **Jack Boettgar** thanks for the argument, which inspired the creation of this drama and later the entire trilogy of novels.

To a fellow bookworm: **Elizabeth Blackwood** for her continued support and encouragement for the completion of my first major writing project. Without her empowerment, I may never have finished my work as rapidly as I did. **Thank You Liz;** for spurring me to keep going forward in my penmanship! I truly appreciate your fortitude on motivating me to strut forward and never giving up on one's dreams of imagination! I am already inspired to pursue my next project in this series. Once more, I say sincerely *Thank you*!

To **all** of my family and associates (*who are still alive*): For any suggestions, corrections, ideas and cheers needed to complete this project!

I want to share a thank you to all my dear readers for your patience and support for the **3½** years it took to write this brainteaser!

Welcome to the first round (*ding*) of a three-part trilogy; see you in the second torturous tournament!

# AUTHOR'S QUICK NOTES

All of us at some time in our lives have played various types of games. No matter where humans are around the world, we enjoy letting loose and have fun playing or creating entertaining tests of skill. As a result, a few people have adapted and adjusted the rules of these sporting events to their everyday lives. Instead of a simple board, card or role-playing game, these individuals go as far as to play psychological contests on various levels, thinking they are the only ones on the top of the heap. As for the rest of humanity, they are nothing but born losers.

For an author who has lived more than 5 decades, I've considered it an honour and a challenge to test my skills at creative writing. Through my years of observation, I've noted that the majority of individuals; whether male or female; seem to run their lives on the little romps they play between the sexes. The conclusions that I arrived at seems to support some sort of unspoken or unwritten rule or regulation that people apply to their personal circumstances, backing up every stratagem they take. On other occasions, breaking those same rules seems to justify that person's ideology, freedom and sense of security during different circumstances.

Now, you may ask what this observer means by his comment above.

Everyone uses psychological contest strategies to obtain what they want when they want it. Whether it requires cutthroat tactics, whining or crying, the outcome of the game is the same; someone wins, others lose. Yet not all games have to be painful or a major financial loss to the individuals involved. Some contest designs are to build up, to encourage or to educate individuals to understand the game play or to be a successful team player. Others hand out rewards to their contestants in the form of moneys or prizes.

Let us take the example of lovers. They use flirting or light teasing to encourage their partner to join in on a romantic liaison; like gentle caressing, holding hands to lightly rubbing their feet together (*playing footsy under a table*), which no one sees them doing. These little loves taps the couple use build up their romance and strengthens their bond of union. Psychologically they are saying how much they love each other and demonstrate it with the action of a kiss or two. However these lovebirds do their romance together, you can guarantee that some sort of recreation is involved, even if it is silently done (*like a wink or a nod*).

Some games promote a challenge to one's intellectual abilities; like puzzles, card games, chess, quizzes and other contests of skill.

Businesses use game stratagems to win their patrons trust and pocketbooks.

Banks use similar strategies to attract more patrons to their financial institutions.

Stock Markets use game rules when stocks go up or drop down, in order to buy or sell stock or bond certificates.

Politicians are another group who win votes by playing different rounds like *'Beat around the Bush,' 'Pass the buck,'* or *'Attack the Opposition'*. They never tell their voters the whole truth and like a game of espionage, they never reveal any details until sometime after events have taken place behind closed doors or they have retired from the public's eyes to write their personal bias memoirs.

Even war games and trying to cheat death are other stratagems to win.

Our list can go on and on and on …

Yes, we humans love to play our recreational contests and skills!

From the time, we are born until death catches up with us, we learn about our society, the world and life in general through the games we employ. The regulations may vary with each person's competition or time, but they are games nonetheless.

The drama that is about to unfold requires some brainpower on your part. As the first round of tournaments begin, keep in the back of your mind one simple question, "***Who really is playing the game?***"

Enjoy the challenge!

*<div align="right">**TRB - 2014!**</div>*

Any reader's questions, comments or book ratings can be shared with the author through the following email address: *thegamemastertrilogy@gmail.com*.

I'd love to hear from yah!

# PROLOGUE

*This is one heck of a morning! The brochure never mentioned a thing about this damp coolness! That is how one could describe it, an ugly, damp coolness, which chills a person to the bone.*

A lone-silhouetted figure walked slowly, beside the shore's edge, thinking. He was wearing a heavy navy-blue cashmere sweater over a white t-shirt, a black toque on his head and old denim jeans.

This individual stopped to absorb the smells and sounds around him. Shaking his head as if in disgust, the wanderer continued his personal reflection of the situation, *to make matters worse, I cannot see more than ten inches in front of me - in any direction.*

Moving forward again, the figure turned to travel up the beach a ways while keeping the sound of the rolling surf, close to his right side.

*Even my flashlight is useless at this early time of the morning.*

In the month of April, the transitional changing weather from the sea could range from tranquil calm to raging fury. Along this portion of the **Pacific Rim** at a location called **Long Beach** on **Vancouver Island**, a territorial terrorist encompassed the entire area – a gloomy **Fog!**

No shoreline, beach, hilltop nor inland forest, close to the sea, was safe from this menace of moisture. For its own amusement, the fog seemed to choke out all visual cues and wreak havoc with a person's senses. Demanding attention by trying to inflict a distorted or silenced envelops over any natural sights and sounds, the fog controlled the battle lines with fervent ease. That is why this stretch of dark, sandy beach could not defend itself from the dominating extortionist. Actually, all of the sandy areas along Long Beach were chocking under the smothering effects of thick white gloom.

Suddenly, a small shaft of orange-red sunlight burst through, just barely penetrating down to the level of the sand. The sunlight's brief charge forward was only momentary. The organized fog surrounded and concealed its prey, overwhelming the beam of sunlight, beating it into submission, until the light vanished as quickly as it had appeared. The fog bank enjoyed its victory with a re-enforcing dance of triumph.

*Something seemed to be there! I thought I saw an outline just over there... Nope! Probably a shadow from ...* Trying to head back to his parked vehicle, the beach-comber tripped over a bleached, debarked, driftwood log that was seen too late to avoid. *Whoa*, falling forward he fell face first into the sandy beach.

*Yuk!* Spitting out sand from his mouth, *I guess coming out to the beach today, was not a brilliant idea*, thought the adventurer.

Standing up and brushing himself off, the hiker continued forward at a much slower pace than before. This was to avoid another log or any other obstacle the retreating tide had deposited along the water's edge that morning.

The Fog's thick talons clamped tightly onto every nook and cranny possible, squeezing like a vice. This made it impossible to see, at times, what lay ahead and seemed to create confusing directions with its flowing fingers of moisture particles bouncing about haphazardly. Even the most powerful fog light could barely cut through this vandal of the senses.

Yet, this foggy tormentor had a powerful enemy to do war with - the radiant **Sun!**

Yes, the unquenchable Sun, rising at the right interval, it knows how to disperse this criminal of the shoreline. Every beam of light, manoeuvred into strategic place, acts as a powerful projectile or a weapon of removal. Slicing, dicing, drilling and hammering silently and relentlessly through the weaknesses of the fog, the Sun poured on its strength minute-by-minute. The sun's rays increased in intensity until this territorial terrorist surrendered, whether peeling away layer by layer or from continuous bombardments, the action was swift and silent.

The lone treasure seeker continued his stroll along the beach. His pace began to quicken to the step of the sun's ever-increasing rhythm, which exposed less and less hazards ahead.

The Morning Sun continued to rise with its shining golden armour, blazing trails of light to fragment and fracture the fog's grip.

As the battle raged on, the man stooped over to look at various items washed up above the shoreline. Totally unaware of this conflict of nature going on around him; he observed pieces of kelp, sea weed strands, broken sea shells, smaller debarked driftwood and these odd coloured glass spheres, with pieces of fishing net still attached to them; strewn about the curved sandy beach.

The fog slowly lifted its sluggish body, while still trying to fight back for the last handhold on its territory.

Picking up the two different sized glass spheres, the scavenger decided to keep them for decorative purposes. *These will add some life to my new cabin*, he thought. Continuing down the beach a ways, the man finally sat down on a large black rock outcrop, examining these two prizes, a little more closely.

A ray of sunlight broke through the battle lines to touch the glass; causing refracting rainbow colours on top the sand's surface, below his feet. *Wow! What a fascinating and colourful effect on the sand!*

The blanket of white continued its ascent upwards. The surrounding scene increased in clarity of focus, as the fog loosened more of its grasp because of the sun's onslaught.

It is now understandable why people called this stretch of coastline Long Beach. The great stretches of multi-coloured sand ran for several miles north and south along the island's ***Pacific Rim National Park's*** western shoreline. Each different coloured concaved beach was broken in a few places by large black rock outcroppings; containing tide pools at sea level and clumps of pine trees on the rock tops; stretched into the Pacific Ocean.

Exposed to the ever-increasing sunlight, occasionally scattered greyish driftwood, along with patches of seaweed strands and the occasional odd shaped rocks decorated these shores during low tide.

As a person looks toward the front lines of pine tree forests, one notices these monstrous trees have their tops bent backwards, as if pointing to the heart of Vancouver Island. These few giants of old age showed they were unable to stand fully erect in a straight line, because of the raging westward winds pressing them inland and smashing the coast line with gargantuan waves of brute strength.

The sun was finally gaining victory over the foggy soup. The scene was clearing much faster as the sun rose higher in the sky. The vanquished villain had no other recourse but to make a hasty retreat - *until next time!*

Getting up again, the lone figure trotted off to a waiting GMC truck on a paved parking lot. Upon opening the door, a large empty mug and a ten-cup thermos of coffee awaited the chilled beachcomber. Finding a place for his two glass trophies, the lone traveler poured coffee into the empty mug and sipped it slowly, watching the victorious sunrise.

The odour of salty sea air combined with the aromas of juniper plants and Pacific Rim Rain Forest; added to the warmth and smell of the coffee. *Boy does this bring back memories,* he thought. As time passed and his memories flowed by, the traveler finally saw the sky clear from the remnants of the war.

Enjoying his freedom was the greatest gift he received. No longer bothered by the divorce from more than ten months earlier, this man of thirty-six enjoyed his multi-millions as he saw fit.

An annoying sound of modern technology disrupted the dreamful thoughts and peacefulness of his mind. Picking up his clunky cell phone, a dreamy "Hello?" sounded.

After a moment of silence while listening to a familiar voice on the other end, a smile crossed his face.

"What took you so long to call me?"

Another pause, then laughter broke out with the following "You haven't figured it out yet? Stumped - Eh?"

After a final long pause, "Sure I will! I would consider it an honour to do so right away." Then a moment later, "Well - when you called, I was traversing down memory lane and reminiscing about …"

# CHAPTER 1

# Family History

The graduates from *Keller's Senior High School,* at *Ben Dover, Utah,* looked forward to the summer of 1938. There would no longer be any more homework! Not even those dumb useless assignments given to them from their teachers. Now was the time to forge forward into the work world or advance oneself with higher education by technical or college courses. Very few of those students looked forward to going to *Yale* or some other university to advance their knowledge. Yet each year, some would take up such a challenge hoping for better jobs in their specific career. Most would drop out within the first two years and head into the work place, never completing their courses. It is for those exceptional few who fight to the reward of completing their career choice that this story begins...

At the Keller's Senior High School, forty-five students were graduating and entering the new challenging world of life before them. Out of forty-five graduates, nine were graduating with 90% averages or also known as - High Honours. Two of these students were **Rupert Body** (*an Americanized shortened name for Vaude van Bodin*) and **Connie Barnes**.

Rupert Body was a slim built, six-foot three-inch, blonde-haired, ocean blue eyed and dashing young man. Most of the girls in his school swooned towards him and could not get enough of his well-defined athletic physique. At times fights had to be broken up amongst the girls who kept bugging him for dates. Yet, with all the attention he received, Rupert never allowed such trappings of teenage hormones to interfere with his studies or his goals for the future.

As for Connie Barnes, she was a five-foot nine-inch fiery-red head with hazel eyes. Her physique was that of a thin, yet shapely modeled - Venus. The boys always whistled to her or said, at times, sexual innuendoes to attract her attention. As a fiery-red head, she knew how to put such sarcastic beggars in their place - verbally. If that did not work, she knew how to put them in the hospital pretty darn quick. Do not back this beauty into any corner, because her temper could slice, dice and fry the appendages off any male suitor. That is how she got the nickname - *The Scarlet Widow*. Most of the boys usually left her alone, except for the ones who kept asking for trouble.

The whole time these two were in high school, neither individual gave any clues or indications of any kind, to any of their friends, that they both truly loved each other. By means of secret hand and body signals; with the occasional coded messages they developed and passed between themselves over the years; Rupert and Connie had their own meeting places selected to share their notes and steal a few loving kisses. Yes, not a single soul knew these two loved each other since they were thirteen years old. Now at the ages of eighteen, both wanted to start their careers first, before committing to marriage to each other. Their love for and respect toward each other was very strong indeed.

These two brilliant individuals could not wait to go to college. Both chose and received acceptance into **Harvard University**. Connie hoped to be a Chemistry Major, while Rupert hoped to be an attorney for any law firm dealing in civil law suits.

After the completion of their first year, Connie realized she had a strong interest in medicine instead of just chemistry and decided to pursue a career as a Registered Nurse or *RN* for short. Her marks at the time averaged 92.64%.

As for Rupert, he realized he had two special gifts or talents he could use instead of learning law. One was the gift of understanding and using complex Trigonometry and Calculus formulas. No matter what the field he worked in, there was always a need for such complex Algebraic formulations. He ended up majoring as a skilled Mathematician with an average around 93.17%.

His second gift was one he explored to the hilt since he was a child. He had the knack of learning complex languages within twenty minutes exposure in amongst different national groups, talking and listening to them as though he had always spoken their language for years. Rupert also had the knack of retaining the languages he quickly obtained and seemed to keep them for up to seven years. If he never used them after seven years, the old adage fell into place; *you do not use it, you will lose it*. Yet if he needed that language again, all Rupert had to do was re-immerse his whole being amongst those languages again and he would pick it up once more. Working in a restaurant that hired various national tongues, Rupert caught on to such languages quickly and rapidly and was nicknamed - *The Linguist*.

Little did each of the romantic lovers realized their choice of career would be a benefit for both of them. Why, you may ask? Times indicated a change in the air of events yet to come. It began with Hitler's march across Europe in 1939 and later amplified with the attack on Pearl Harbour in 1941.

World War II took its toll on people, lives and property. Connie volunteered and used her career to help those on the front lines with medical assistance. The American Government snatched up Rupert to work as a translator and cryptographer. This was because of his quickness in learning different languages and his mathematical skills.

Neither party saw each other again until October of 1945. Upon meeting once more, after so many years apart, their love grew more powerful than when they were in high school or university. It was at this point; both decided to marry as soon as they could. Their marriage took place in July of 1946 and they finally known as Mr. and Mrs. Body.

Life sure was tough after World War II ended for the newly married couple. After two years, they settled into their daily routine of married life. They prepared to become a family with children. Rupert thought that his wife should have the honour of naming their future children; although Connie insisted that her husband name any boys that came along.

Mrs. Body gave birth to their firstborn son on February 14th, 1950, and named him - *Calvin Archer Body*. It was an easy way to remember his name; both parents used the idea of naming their son with a hidden three-lettered pet name. The idea came from their early years, during their senior school days, passing cryptic messages to each other. [*Connie preferred to call Calvin - 'Cabby' for short*].

If any further children came in the future, the parents used the same trick and it became the child's pet name. Yet, unbeknown to these parents, these pet names seemed to indicate, almost prophetically, what kinds of careers their children would have, or personality types they would become, in the future. For Example: Calvin's first job was a cab driver, which he drove for six years. Later, Calvin took on the career as a jeweller, through his expertise in lapidary work making cabs of stones and setting them into various gold, silver and platinum settings.

By taking turns at baby-sitting his younger siblings; Calvin developed such exceptional fatherly skills, that when he married at the age of 20, he carried this knowledge over to the next generation. Such fine qualities came from his observations of how his parents raised and trained him.

Within two years, Mrs. Body gave birth to their next child, a daughter named *Shirley Ursula Body* on May 19th, 1952. She became a substitute teacher for various schools around her county when she got older. Her expertise helped to educate or train other teachers and principals on how to handle the children in an ever-changing future.

She got married at the age of 21 to a man of mercantile expertise. Though they never had any children of their own, 13 years later, Shirley eventually divorced her spouse in order to live a freer life. She never married again! Later, she died in a plane crash, over Florida. She was 44 years old.

On July 23rd, 1954, another son was born - **_Taze Atlas Body_**.

His name says it all! Taze definitely became a tabloid writer and a celebrity gossipmonger. The family usually tolerated him for his sleazy news collecting, yet they avoided revealing too much about themselves to him. Warping and twisting the truth in any convenient direction possible, a person never knew if they would become the target or inadvertent source of Taze's next gossip column. His columns made him such fame, that he moved up through the ranks of the newspaper, from writer to assistant chief editor in a period of 29 years.

Gossip was Taze's way of life! If a person thought that they could hide some juicy tidbit of information, this news hound smelled it out quickly. No concealed nook, cranny or dark alley could obscure information from his muzzle. If Taze thought there was a news item to find, he always found it. This nearly cost him his life on three occasions. Sniffing too hard and too long could get a person killed. Yet Taze was the rough and tumble type. Nothing stopped him.

Taze did marry one gorgeous female performer when he was 23. The two of them had three wonderful children together. Their marriage was on a concrete foundation that lasted them until 1999. Taze had a major heart attack and he was unable to make it to the hospital on time. His life ended abruptly, at the age of 45.

Finally on August 11th, 1956, their second daughter was born - ***Rose Olive Body***.

She was the one daughter with a big chip on her shoulders, by always playing the victim role to get attention. Rose's major weaknesses were the street skills she learned and acquired while in the wrong crowd; called pick pocketing. She also had a psychological problem with fast fingers - kleptomania - that always got her in trouble and on the wrong side of the law.

Rupert had bailed Rose out of jail once too often, for his taste. The constant run-ins with the law finally stretched his nerves to the point of no return. It broke his heart to see his favourite daughter go through these continual ordeals. The result was his eventual refusal to help her and let her face the consequences for her actions. This last straw finally worked.

Getting the help she needed, through psychological therapy and counselling, Rose eventually stopped becoming a thief. She married a wealthy entrepreneur and straightened her life around at the age of 26. Rose went as far as to incorporate her pick-pocketing skills, into entertaining magic trick shows for the local children. Rose had raised four beautiful children and remains happily married to her loyal, loving husband.

All four of the Body children had average marks in school, between 71 to 76%. Even though their marks were not as high as their parents were, their parents loved them for their brilliance and completion of all twelve grades of school.

As for Rupert, he stayed with the American Government. His employment continued as a skilled translator and cryptographer during the Korean and Vietnam Wars. He and his family continually moved across the grand United States, until settling in Red Bluff, Northern California, in late 1963.

Rupert died of heart failure in September 21st, 1977, at the age of 57 and left his widow a considerably large governmental death benefits package. This was to keep Connie going, for the rest of her life.

Since the death of her husband, Connie had an opportunity in 1978 to re-educate herself into becoming a doctor. She took on this challenging task and continued her medical profession, as a doctor, until she retired at the age of 67.

Connie never got married again. The reason why, she figured she had had the best of the crop and no longer saw the need to remarry. Besides, she had thirteen wonderful grandchildren to spoil.

She lived until August 1st, 1993. It happened in the middle of the night. A brain haemorrhage killed her unexpectedly and swiftly.

Both love birds left behind five beautiful children to carry on the family legacy and traditions.

# CHAPTER 2

# Genius by Design!

It was late in January, when Rupert and Connie Body decided to go out for an early anniversary dinner together, without their children. It was definitely a romantic situation with plenty of love in the air. Hiring their eldest son for the baby-sitting job, both parents wanted a quiet evening together. This was not always an easy thing to do, since the parents never knew what their kids were always up too while they had their night out.

As for the Body's evening together, it seemed that every time they tried to have it on their anniversary date, some silly child's accident or annoying job situation would interfere with their dinner plans. This resulted in their having it postponed as late as three months after their actual anniversary date. This New Year was going to be different! They unanimously decided to start it super early in the year and enjoy the time they could have when all seemed quiet.

For the first time in many years, this was the first anniversary that went through without a hitch. Nevertheless, the romance never ended on that evening. Rupert and Connie in one week had enjoyed romantic sexual interludes that they

9

had not done for quite a few years. This presented a challenge since the children were always around and seemed to add a rush of excitement to their sexual escapades. Besides, they have the right to do this, since they are married to each other!

It was in the middle of the month of February that the sickness every morning showed up. Thinking at first, she had caught a severe case of Influenza, Connie ended up not going to work for a few weeks. She hoped this bug in her system would quit its rampage and nauseating effects. Finally, at the beginning of March, she went to their family doctor were the truth came out. Connie was not sick with any persistent Flu bug. Instead, she was pregnant with their fifth child.

Although such news was unexpected, both parents were happy and hoped this would be their last child. They were willing to accept a boy, a girl or even the remote possibility of twins. As long as the child was healthy, they just knew that nine months down the road, their fifth child would arrive.

= = =

During the time of Connie's pregnancy, Rupert got the unexpected chance to move up in the governmental work force. Unfortunately, the job opening was a limited position and the responsible recipient would have to move to Northern California, to work in the new department there. The competition for this position was fierce and Rupert's chances were slim indeed, since he was competing with 27 others. Yet, hoping against all odds, to get the new position with higher pay, Rupert put his name in anyway.

In the month of June, Rupert seemed to beat all the odds and was one of the top three finalists for the new job. He had second place and beaten by a colleague of his who lived on Rhode Island - *Charles (Chuck) Sanderson*. The third place individual was someone he did not know and lived in New Orleans.

The idea of moving did not appeal to his kids. They had all their friends to give up and start fresh all over again. If their dad did have this job, it would mean that they would have to move again - for the sixth time. Rebellion from Rupert's children seemed to run rampant that early summer. Not until he sat down and explained to them what would happen, they had to wait to see if he did get the new position in the government.

To the joy of the children, on the 12th of August, Rupert got the news through a telegram that his colleague, Charles got the job. Not too surprised at the choice, Rupert just continued on, as he did before. He was extremely happy that Chuck got the assignment and he could not wait to congratulate him, for his success, as soon as possible. Little did Rupert realize that that was the last time he would ever speak to his friend and colleague Charles again!

Five weeks later Charles (Chuck) Sanderson died in a single engine plane crash. He was traveling through the Rockies, in Washington State, when a lightning storm brewed up without warning. Charles lost his direction and being unable to see clearly through the turbulent rainfall, ended up smashing his small plane into a solid rock face. The disaster was unavoidable. Chuck expired instantly.

To lose a close colleague affected Rupert for several months after the funeral.

Since being informed about Chuck's death, Rupert reluctantly, but willingly took on this new challenging position. He had to make the necessary preparations for his family's move to come. The big move was to begin December 10th, despite the continuous objections of his unruly children.

= = = = =

The Body family arrived at the **Billings General Hospital** in **Billings**, **Montana**. Leaving his uncle's home in a hurry, Rupert drove Connie to the hospital due to her increasing birthing pains. Connie was expecting her fifth child after six hours of increased labour. It did not matter to her if the child was another boy or girl, just as long as it was a healthy one. Her baby was preparing to push its way into the world.

While the Body family was in the hospital, this was also a special day for the people in Dallas, Texas. The President of the United States was due to arrive aboard his Air Force One Jet.

The labour pains dramatically increased in the last 30 minutes. "How soon can I get rid of this watermelon!" exclaimed Connie.

The President's Jet finally landed, taxied to and came to a complete stop before a staircase, and a rolled out red carpet.

The pain intervals continued to intensify. She clenched her husband's hand so tightly, that the tips of his fingers began turning various shades of blue and purple. Connie shouted at her husband, "I hate you for this! ... You did this to me! ... This better be the last one! .... I don't want to go through this ever again - HEAR ME!" between each contraction. Rupert Body just only cringed from the pain in his hand, caused from his wife's vice-like grip.

When the door opened, the President and his wife came out of the Air Force 1. Smiling and waving to a small crowd, they headed down the staircase to their motorcade, which was waiting for them, at the end of the red carpet. Dallas' Mayor and his wife, shaking hands and exchanging greetings with each other, met them at the motorcade. A small girl stepped forward, curtsying to the president's wife and handing her a beautiful, large bouquet of roses.

Suddenly, Connie's water broke. It sent a torrent of water cascading to the floor. The child was now in the proper position, forcing its way out into the world.

As soon as Rupert could yank his hand free between a set of contractions, the president's motorcade started on route to their scheduled luncheon.

Rupert shook his hand to get the feeling and blood to come back into his fingers. The child's head was crowning.

More voters flooded to the motorcade route smiling and waving. Some people wanted to give flowers to the president's wife as they drove by, but the police barricade lines prevented that from happening. Others tried to run ahead of the motorcade, squeezing through the thinner crowd lines for a better view of the parade passing them by. One man had an epileptic seizure and collapsed onto the side of the road. An ambulance hauled him away.

Pushing again, the child's head finally came out, stopping at the shoulders. Heavy breathing sounds came from Connie.

Returning smiles and waves, the President, the Mayor and their wives continued their parade on Main Street through the city of Dallas, Texas, heading for Houston Street.

The man with the seizure was collected off the street and taken by ambulance to the nearest hospital. The motorcade turned left off Main Street onto Houston Street.

Exhausted, but determined, Connie wanted to complete this nine-month agony. Encouraged by everyone present in the maternity ward, she took several deep breaths to push the rest of the child's body out into the doctor's waiting arms.

It was at this point, of the final push; that the President's motorcade was on Houston Street and heading for Elm Street, which the child came out at 12: 28 P.M. CST (*Central Standard Time*).

"It's a boy!" announced the doctor. Working fast before the doctor cleared the nasal passages of the baby. There was a problem. The boy was not breathing and no vocal response came from his tiny vocal cords!

At 12:30 P.M., rounding the corner onto Elm Street, the motorcade continued its parade for all the scattered spectators there. Within seconds, gunshots began to ring out.

The doctor lifted the child by its feet to swat it on the buttocks. At the same moment the President of the United States, followed by the Dallas Mayor, had been hit by flying lead.

As the doctor's hand proceeded to make contact with the child's buttocks, was the exact moment that the *fatal shot* killed the President of the United States.

It seemed that as one life force rapidly departed from one individual; another life force became infused into the newly born baby boy. Gasping in his first breath, the baby screamed the most ear shattering and heart-wrenching shriek that any human had ever heard before. This cry of havoc chilled every one present to the bone. Almost losing his grip on the newborn due to this terrifying sound, the doctor looked at the nearby nurse and parents. All became unexpected silence.

*What was that all about*, thought the doctor!

Tying off and then cutting the umbilical cord, the doctor handed the baby to the nurse to wash and wrap him in a small blue blanket.

The President's motorcade sped off to the local Dallas Texas Hospital with the presidents' lifeless body; while in Montana, a new child became an active animated person.

The healthy baby weighed in at 8 lbs 8 oz.

This new one had finally calmed down since his first breath. Wrapped up in a small blanket to keep him warm, and placed into his waiting mother's arms, he was sleeping soundly and sucking on his tiny thumb.

"Have you found a name for your new family member?" asked the doctor.

"Yes", exclaimed Mr. Body with great joy, "his name will be **Noah Oscar Body!**"

Noah's mother smiled and nodded an agreement to this name.

Kissing his wife and then little newborn Noah, Rupert exclaimed, "Welcome to a strange new world - my son! . . ."

While a hard working family gained a new and (*unknown at this time*) unique family member, a traumatic change of events took place on this day, leaving America realizing, she had lost her innocence - forever!

The Date: November 22nd, 1963!

CHAPTER 3

# What happened?

As an infant, baby Noah hardly cried vocally. He was an exceptionally quiet baby, compared to his older siblings, when they were his age. When changing Noah's diapers, he would suck on his tiny toes or hands, from time to time. Sleeping was not a problem for Noah, he had the ability to sleep through the worst raging storms, whenever they hit. At feeding time, he quietly enjoyed his meals and would often try to mimic his mother's smile and facial expressions.

As he grew, little redheaded Noah showed signs of inquisitive alertness. He enjoyed observing his world around him whenever his mother took him out on strolls through the parks or walks down town. Each time they were out together, he silently took in these new surroundings with wide questioning hazel eyes. The vastness of the vivid colours sounds and motion kept his little mind awake and alert until they arrived back home. Seeming to always be a happy and contented little tyke, 'Nobby'[1] loved the world scenes around him.

---

[1]   Go to appendix "A" for more information.

At home, when he was put to bed for a siesta in the afternoon, little '*Nobby*' would fall asleep quickly and sleep for a minimum of 2 hours.

Like any family, with more than one child, the children of the Body family formed various alliances (*or bonding*) with other members. Shirley and Taze had a unique closeness; they both enjoyed sharing the latest secret or gossip about anyone or anything. These two would disappear for short time periods in order to exchange or compare notes. Upon returning, they acted as if they did not want to be around each other. As hard as both scoundrels tried to disguise their brown nosing techniques for newsgathering, their little skits never fooled their parents.

Calvin began developing a bond with his youngest brother Noah. From the time this little tyke was home from the hospital, Calvin wanted his turn at taking care of or holding him. Although this seemed awkward at first, his parents were mind-boggled to see such loving concern from their oldest son. Yet, here was an opportunity for Calvin to learn fatherly skills. By taking a turn caring for and defending little Noah, Calvin protected the tyke from the others and their antics. Besides, is it not the responsibility of the oldest to set the example for the other family members? Calvin thought so! He demonstrated this quality by willingly baby-sitting little Noah when necessary.

The Body family had other members added to them - besides children. There was **Squeak** the hamster, **Goldie** the gold fish, **Badger** and **Walkie-Talkie** - a pair of chattering budgies. These pets kept the children entertained and helped them to demonstrate their skills of responsibility, even though the parents ended up doing most of the work and not the kids.

Their most outstanding pet, while every one's favourite, was **Mizer**, a five-year-old, tabby-mix tomcat. This feline loved the game of chasing strings or old ties across the floor. Whenever this happened, Mizer seemed to become like a little kitten again, full of energy, with lots of life.

He would use various hunting techniques on his prey; sneaking around stealthily, coiling up into a small ball only to spring or pouncing forward; running away only to attack from another direction or from under the couch - sideways.

During such playtime, Mizer displayed his effective cat skills of attack or retreat. Otherwise, he loafed around to conserve energy (*as all cats do*), ate his favourite canned cat cuisine and was happy having a family who takes care of his every need and whim. Remember, this feline is the master of this home and not the humans.

One time while watching over his youngest brother, Calvin observed a competition that occurred between their house cat, Mizer and Noah. He was at the kitchen table writing out an essay for school homework. Taking a break at that time, before finishing his assignment, Calvin noted the time was 4:07 PM. Keeping silent, he watched the following development take place.

Mizer was lying down comfortably in his favourite chair in the living room. He happened to open his green slit eyes and observed Noah playing on top of the couch with a few of his toys. When Noah, only 6 months old at the time, sensed watchful eyes on him, stopped his playing. Tilting his head up, looking around the living room, he first looked left and then panning his head slowly to the right. Noah stopped briefly to glare at Calvin, who waved at him silently. Nevertheless, this tyke's radar told his senses he was still under observation but not by his older brother. Continuing his pan to the right, Noah locked his hazel eyes on Mizer's green-slit ones.

The staring contest began with non-blinking eyes. The object of this battle was for each combatant to try to make the other submit and give up the game. The one who blinks their eyes first is the loser. Mizer, who enjoyed this game of staring down others; whether human or fellow pets; swished the last third of his tail calmly from side to side as though indicating a confident win, in two minutes or less.

Without interrupting, Calvin decided to time this event, massaging his tired hands and waited.

As six-minute mark arrived and left, Mizer began to slow down the swishing of his tail. As for Noah, still not blinking, he continued his staring as if to ask the question, "what do you want of me?"

The tail stopped moving around the nine-minute mark. Mizer decided at this point, to sit up a little higher than before to make this puny human submit to his control.

Sensing the possibility of danger to his little friend, Calvin prepared quietly to angle his chair for a quick dash, to collect the toddler from the slashing razor sharp claws of Mizer. Noah, in the meantime, remained like a fixed statue, not moving or reacting to anything else except glaring at the feline's green slit eyes.

Around the eleven-minute mark, Mizer's tail began an up and down slapping motion that started slowly and progressed rapidly. It seemed to indicate the cat's annoyance to the little person for not submitting to his stare.

By the Fifteen-minute mark, Mizer could not handle the competition any longer. Jumping down to the floor, the tabby-mix made a clipped *"Row"* sound and aristocratically strutted off. With his head held high, tail in the air, pointing and swivelling his backside to Noah Mizer displayed his defiant attitude toward his competitor. This feline enjoyed showing how much contempt he had for the child and for the loss of the staring contest. Noah, on the other hand, continued to stare at the back of Mizer while the cat left the room and was out of sight. Once gone, Noah went back to playing with his toys again.

As for Calvin, all he did was breathe a sigh of relief, chuckled quietly to no one and went back to completing his school assignment. Later, at dinnertime, Calvin told the whole family about what had happened.

While everyone laughed and congratulated Noah for winning, poor Mizer jumped down from his hiding spot on the top of the fridge and sauntered out the cat door. To lose a staring contest to a child is one thing, but to have his nose rubbed in about the loss was another situation altogether. Mizer stayed out all-night and refused to come home when called by either Rupert or Connie.

One of these future days, he was going to get even with Noah for losing the staring contest.

= = =

As time went by, little *'Nobby'* learned to crawl, walk and later to talk earlier than toddlers do his age. Seeming to be always a happy and a contented little tyke, Noah loved the world of motion and action around him. Like a game, Noah always found something new to examine or explore.

In the Body's backyard, Connie grew a few flowers to decorate the landscape in various sized Rock Gardens. Most times when she was hanging out the wash, little *'Nobby'* would travel around the yard; explore all the beautiful flowers and insects that buzzed around. This kept him entertained for hours.

One day, when Connie finally finished hanging up some bed sheets to dry on a clothesline, she sat down for a short break to keep an eye on her little *'Nobby'*. She was not the only pair of eyes observing the little human.

Mizer, who loved sun tanning on top of the lean-to garage roof, also watched the child's antics. He found this the safest place to hide from the toddler. They did not get along with each other. Noah did not understand that petting a cat was a gentle action, not with a hard whacking pat or pulling hard with a clenched fist of fur.

Squealing with delight, sixteen-month-old Noah chased various butterflies around the backyard. Although it was harder to do than it looked, this new game of trying to catch a Monarch Butterfly (*or any flying insect like dragonflies or moths*) kept him entertained. Try with all of his strength to catch the beautiful insect; Noah seemed to miss his mark, stumbling twice in his pursuit. Not allowing the small flying creatures to outdistance him, *'Nobby'* continued to pursue his prey. The

Monarch desperately tried to gain altitude through a technique of twisting and turning in an aerodynamic ballet. The butterfly flew higher in the air to avoid this giant predator on two legs.

Connie could not get over her youngest son's energy. He seemed determined to catch that butterfly no matter what. While Connie's energy levels dropped, trying to maintain a happy home with all her chores, her youngest kept her hopping more than her older children did at this age. Just to have a quick break and observing her son's antics brought back a flood of fond memories. All of her children at one time or another played this chasing game around the backyard. Usually the others gave up after half an hour of running around. Not her Nobby, he could do this for an hour, none stop, if given the chance.

After a thirty-nine minute chase, Noah stopped chasing the butterfly only to watch it fly up and over the roof of the house. The fanciful creature disappeared from view. Realizing his mother was watching him; Noah just pointed and made a sad face. He looked like he was going to cry. His fun game ended too soon for him.

Connie raced over to her son and picked him up. Having her son's full attention, Connie talked to him and consoled the lad, so he would not cry.

"That's ok, Nobby. The butterfly will be back again! You'll see him tomorrow." Then Connie gave a kiss to her youngest child.

Noah began to yawn and rub his tiny hazel eyes. He was determined to continue his game. Unfortunately, his little body told his mind he needed a nap because of burning too much energy. After the rest, he would have his batteries recharged to continue his test of skills.

Unknown to this mother and son relationship, the same butterfly flew around the other side of the house and fluttered toward the two humans.

The Monarch flew past Mizer, who tried to catch the insect with his paw. Although he nearly fell off the roof trying, Mizer was not close enough to catch it. Therefore, he decided to watch where it would land, only to attack it later.

In a quick moment, the butterfly fluttered and then landed on Noah's little nose.

Connie was startled to see the butterfly come from out of nowhere. Without moving, she watched it land.

The insect's tiny feet tickled the tyke and made him sneeze and rub his tiny nose.

Connie watched the Monarch fly away when her '*Nobby*' sneezed.

"Yuk", exclaimed Noah, "it kissed me!"

Both of them laughed together as the Monarch arched and dived to softly land on a Daisy flower ten feet away.

Mizer saw his chance. This seven-year-old feline climbed off the garage roof to seek up on his new prey.

Noah again began rubbing his eyes.

"It's bedtime for you - sleepyhead!"

"No", objected little '*Nobby*'. He tried to force his eyes to stay open, without yawning and wiggling out of mother's strong arms.

Noah continued his objections, crying, until after his little head hit the pillow. He rubbed and closed his little hazel eyes for his afternoon siesta. Within seconds, Noah was sound asleep in dreamland.

As for Mizer, he missed his second opportunity of catching that fluttering Monarch. It flew away before he could sneak up to it. Then Mizer decided to chase the other insects for a while. He caught a Blue Bottle Housefly instead and ate it.

Mizer continued his predatory offensive manoeuvres, looking and acting like a little kitten. He quit after fifteen minutes of fun because his stomach said it was lunchtime.

# CHAPTER 4

# The Quick Start Method

"I **hate** that little podgy brat! He gets all of the attention. I'm the one who is important, not that squealing piglet," exclaimed Rose one day. She did not like her youngest brother. "All he does is take the attention away from me," she stated to Taze. Therefore, she formulated her revenge by doing mean things to this new family member.

On one occasion, after school, *Robby* stole all of Noah's little toy building blocks, while he was playing with them. Making the mom's little '*Nobby*' cry was her ultimate pleasure and goal in life. Yet despite her cruel efforts to upset the tyke, Noah could have cried out in anger by screaming at the top of his little lungs.

Instead of upsetting the tyke, he thought his sister was playing a new version of the game Hide and Seek. He laughed and crawled around to various areas in the living room looking for his missing blocks. *This is fun*, thought Noah, *I will find out where you hid them*.

When Calvin came home five minutes later, he could not figure out why his friend Noah was wandering around looking for something lost. Pegging down Rose, like the Spanish Inquisitor, he found out what she had done to Noah. Later that evening, Rose received severe discipline by her father for her antics. *I'm going to make him pay for it for the rest of his life*; she planned, *for stealing the attention I was supposed to get.*

This bout of anger from *Robby,* towards *Nobby,* had raged on for six more years. Then it stopped at a time when she began to change into a teenager. Every time she tried different cruel things to Noah, his growing optimistic mind thought she was teaching him a new game and he was trying to figure out her rules.

As Noah got older, his interest in life and the world around him blossomed. The more he learned, the more he wanted to learn. His mind was like a sponge that was never full to satisfaction; he had to continue to fill it with more and more data. Constantly playing games with him, the family had educated this nurturing mind to enjoy life and meet head on with the problems that could crop up. Noah's way of tackling a problem was to apply the rules of any game to find the solution, at the same time enjoying the challenge.

By the age of three, Noah was able to say his ABC's and count up to the number ten (*although he sometimes missed the numbers seven and four*). He also was starting to make full sentences, earlier than most children did his age. This caught the attention of his parents and they wondered if their little 'Nobby' was more intelligent than he looked for his age. They wanted to find out if their youngest son was gifted child. Was there a quick start method of educating this youngster, sooner than other children?

After psychological specialists did several tests with the young boy, they informed his parents that Noah was indeed a smart lad, possibly bordering on a level of a genius. Although it was still too early for them to tell, the doctors encouraged Connie and Rupert to go ahead and educate their son to read, write, draw and even learn music. The boy's quick mind was able to pick up and retain the information taught to him, especially when the education was in the form of a game.

One of the things his parents did was to teach their son to read. Not only was he having the joy of his favourite children's books read to him, but he was also learning, in time, how to read those same books by himself.

Noah's mind sponged in everything he was learning. He picked up and retained the distinctions between the different words and their meanings. If he did not understand a word, his inquisitive mind would request the meaning of that word and a repetition of the word's pronunciation. Noah grasped many words and their meanings from both of his parents and his older brother Calvin.

By 1969, *Flower Power Children* ruled everywhere. They had a carefree and sex free lifestyle, during a time when man made the scientific impossibility become a reality – humans landing on the moon, collecting moon rocks and returning home safely.

The *Flower Power Children* also danced to the music of many rock and roll bands like the Beatles or the Beach Boys. Nevertheless, change was on its way!

The decade of the 1970's developed a more conservative ideology on life and life style. The attitude toward the Flower

Power Children developed into a pessimistic atmosphere, which prevailed over the industrialized nations toward such free loading individuals.

During this period, the *Richard Nixon Watergate Scandal* broke out, while the US pulled their troops out of and ending the *Vietnam War* in 1972. By the middle of the 70's, the stock markets took a major Bear nosedive downwards and its ripple effects showed up in different ways. As for Hollywood, they cashed in on these negative vibes by producing movies with disaster, horror or war type themes to them: Such as *Airport* series, *Jaws*, *Towering Inferno* and even *Star Wars*. Some movies both entertained people and made large profits for the movie industries bigwigs despite the down movement of the markets. Gasoline, groceries and restaurant prices slowly soared upwards to compensate for the economy's falling trend.

When Noah entered into grade one, his inquisitive mind continued to absorb and accelerate faster than his fellow students. His method for success was the continued encouragement of his parents to read and search for his own answers to life. He also developed a speed-reading habit and a photographic memory, which enabled him to remember everything he read.

By grade five, Noah was almost at a grade eight level of understanding the world around him. He was also at the same level of comprehension of complex mathematical calculations.

By the age of thirteen, Noah entered **Red Bluff Regional High School** in **Red Bluff, California**, at a grade ten level. He found school way to easy and boring for his ever-expanding and inquisitive mind. Through his own research, he came upon a concept that could predict the up and down trends of the stock market almost accurately. Talking to his father about his research project and his forecast for the future stock market, Noah asked if he could borrow money to test out his theory. Although hesitant at first, Rupert finally saw his son's enthusiasm for this scheme and reluctantly gave $600.00 towards Noah's plans. Noah had squirreled away an additional $350.00 in his small piggy bank hidden in his bedroom (*a piggy bank his sister Robby never found out about*). He combined the two amounts of moneys in order to invest in the stock market and wait for the next great Bull Run to begin.

A week later, Rupert died not knowing whether his youngest son's forecasted plans succeeded or not.

Eleven days after his father's funeral, Noah received his first insight about bullies.

***Shawn Baron*** was the worst bully in Senior High. Even though he made it to grade twelve, his poor skills in reading and writing left him at a level of a grade seven student. He always loved his sports and excelled in this field, but his academic skills left him lagging behind. Therefore, his favourite sport was picking on the brainiest or shortest kids in school. He forced them to do his homework or receive a pummelling. This allowed him more time to concentrate on winning the various football and hockey games he played.

It was the beginning of October, while on a class break, that Noah had his first run in with Shawn. Noah just finished collecting his books for his next two classes, when he felt two sets of hands slammed him into his closed locker. Turning around to see who did this stupid action, Noah came face-to-face with

Shawn's gang of bullies, known as the **Hacksaw Barons**. They surrounded Noah and prevented him from heading off to his next classes.

"So", emphasized Shawn, "You're the brainy midget in this school? Tell me '*Brains*', if you are so smart, why are you not doing my homework? I need to pass my next history class exam or I risk failing my grade twelve. What do you say about that?"

Noah quickly surveyed his opponents. "No", he stated calmly, "Do your own homework."

Shawn's anger rose, as he pushed Noah into the locker to emphasize his point, "You're going to do my history lessons or else. '*Pow*' right in the kisser."

**Roger Hacksaw**, Shawn's brainless second-in-command, piped up, "Yeah! We'll beat you to a pulp – Punk!" The rest of the **Hacksaw Barons** agreed with Roger.

Noah directed his statement to Shawn while ignoring the rest of the gang. "You would never benefit from someone else's work. Besides, how will you succeed in the world having others do your work for you?"

"Because I say so," demanded Shawn, while re-pushing Noah into his locker.

Noah thought for a moment. Looking straight into his opponent's light-green eyes, he challenged him to a test of the mind. "I may do what you demand, if you can give me the answers to four mathematical questions: (1) how do you get four 6's to total …"

"What shit is this? You're going to do what I say …", but Shawn's sentence was cut midway.

"Let the cute kid talk," stated Sandra, Shawn's blonde haired girlfriend. She pinched Noah's left cheek at the same time. When Noah's cheek turned red, she let it go, laughing like any other airhead. The other girls laughed with her!

Directing his statement to Shawn only, Noah began, "If you want me to do as **you** requested, you'll first have to find the answers to these four questions. If you cannot find the answers before the exam date of Friday next week, then you will **never** demand of me or anyone else - anything - ever again. Understand?"

"Well," thought Shawn as he released the kid. "Give me your retarded questions. But if I get them before Friday of next week, you'll do exactly as I say – right?"

"To a certain degree," stated Noah in a rough agreement.

Pushing Noah against the locker again, "You better agree or enjoy being in the hospital for the rest of your life," snickered Shawn.

"Fair enough," Noah calmly exclaimed.

"Excellent," exclaimed Shawn.

The rest of the *Hacksaw Barons* snickered, knowing that Noah was not going to win against this strong willed bully.

"Here are my four questions again:

1.  *How do you get four 6's to total the sum of 30?*[2]
2.  *How do you get five 5's to total the sum of 6?*
3.  *How do you get seven 7's to total the sum of 100?*
4.  *How do you get five 8's to total the sum of 2?* "

---

[2]   Could you answer these four questions? If not, go to Appendix "B".

Shawn let go of the kid and started to think.

Some of the gang watched Shawn's reactions, hoping for a clue from their leader to beat someone up. The rest puzzled over the questions.

Looking confused and annoyed, Shawn requested that Noah write down the questions.

Noah obliged.

He wrote out the following: 6, 6, 6 & 6 = 30 at the top of a piece of paper. Next, he wrote 5, 5, 5, 5 & 5 = 6 in the middle of that same piece of paper. On the top of the back of the paper, Noah wrote out 7, 7, 7, 7, 7, 7 & 7 = 100. In the middle, he wrote 8, 8, 8, 8 & 8 = 2.

The other gang members began scratching their heads, looking dumbstruck at each other, as if unable to solve this mess. Finally, after three minutes, Roger asked for a hint.

Noah asked with sarcasm, "You guys want a hint, so soon!"

Delaying in giving the hint, Noah finally said, "Ok! Ok! When you use one number, cross it off from the list, until all the numbers are finished. Do not add any other numbers just use what numbers that are given. Have fun solving such complicated enigmas!"

Noah left his opponents by the locker arguing over the possible answers to the questions and headed off to his next class.

Shawn and the Hacksaw Barons never did figure out the solutions to the questions. This infuriated the gang leader and he wanted to get revenge on 'Brains' as soon as possible.

While the Hacksaw Barons picked on some other kids and left 'Brains' alone, Shawn was not satisfied with his agreement with Brains. So he schemed a way to get even with Noah and make him pay for his refusal to submit to his demands.

In order to win and control this midget freak '*Brains*', Shawn had to play a more powerful mind game back on Noah.

Three weeks after barely passing his history exam, Shawn entered the school library and tried to find a book of puzzles or complicated mathematical equations. He was searching for a way to even the score with Noah for what happened five weeks prior. He found what he was looking for. He copied out the question and memorized the answer (*a task not easy for this athletic mind*).

"Now to get that brat," he exclaimed under his breath.

Waiting for the right moment, Shawn, without the Hacksaw Barons, found Noah and pounced on him, during the morning class break.

"So you think you are so smart – Eh? Well here is a question for you. If you answer it correctly, I will never bother you again. If you are unable to answer this question, you will be my slave until the end of this year."

"We've already gone over this. You agree never to bother me again. This was sworn by you in front of your gang members", replied Noah.

"Listen punk! This one is between you and me. If you refuse to answer this question, you will automatically be my slave – boy. So you better answer it," as Shawn pushed Noah into the lockers.

"Alright – all right," stated Noah, "Show me what you got."

Shawn let go of the boy and handed him a piece of paper. On it was the following words:

*A French Baker, by the last name of Bordeaux, in May of 1940, had an extra-ordinary week of sales. When he opened his shop for the last time on a Friday morning, customers and cash flowed in, while baked goods flooded off the shelves and out the shop doors. The baker sold just about everything in his bakeshop by 10:38 am. The reason he sold so much product in so little time was that the German forces were marching towards Paris and ready to conquer the capital - Paris. Out of all the products, he sold that morning, only nine beautiful long French loaves of white bread remained. Since the baker no longer needed the extra staff that day, he let them all go home early, while he continued to watch over his bakeshop.*

*Not sure if he was able to sell these last items before noon, ten customers came rushing in at 10:55 am. They needed a loaf of bread immediately. Mr. Bordeaux was more than willing to accommodate these customers; the only problem was he had just nine loaves left instead of ten. Since he ran out of flour earlier that day, he would be unable to make any more loaves until possibly after the war (or if his bakeshop was still standing).*

*The customers bickered over who should get a loaf and who should not. Tempers flew and the baker had a major challenge to calm everyone down. The high stress levels were rampant in the air due to the threat of the German invasion soon to arrive. Ordering everyone present to be silent, the baker carried the nine loaves to his kitchen counter. Laying the loaves out in three rows of three loaves, he puzzled over this dilemma. After five minutes, Mr. Bordeaux finally came up with a possible solution to the problem.*

*[At this point in the story, the average person would consider that cutting off one-tenth of each loaf would achieve the desired*

*effect. If a person did not mind eating all heals (or crusts) then this would have accommodated the request. However, to make the divisions fare, no one individual could receive all heals (or crusts) of the bread.]*

*Therefore, Mr. Bordeaux devised a way to portion out and wrapped up each loaf in such a manner that each customer received a loaf of bread. Leaving satisfied the customers paid for their loaf and left the bakery. As for the baker, Mr. Bordeaux turned over the closed sign on his shop door, locking the doors, pulled down the blinds by 11:59 am.*

*How did this French Baker accommodate his final customers in distributing the nine loaves evenly amongst ten workingmen? What are the correct portions of bread Mr. Bordeaux came up with so each worker received his individual loaf?[3]*

**Hint**: *Remember, each person has to receive at least two heals of bread.*

"You have until the end of the lunch hour to give me an answer," stated Shawn.

Noah read the paper through and something about the question that seemed to strike a chord. Staring off into space, his grey cells clicked furiously, traveling at speeds beyond light. Searching through every archive, nook and cranny of knowledge stored inside his brain, these grey cells scanned for that allusive answer ... when suddenly ... the answer was right before his eyes.

"I have it!"

---

[3]   If you received this question, could you calculate out the equation? A clue may await you in Appendix "C".

Writing the answer out, Noah handed the paper back to Shawn. It contained the correct answer. Turning without saying another word, Noah headed off to class.

Shawn stood there stupefied as he watched GM leave. The kid gave him the correct answer in less than five minutes. *How does he do it*, he pondered. Shaking his head in disbelief, Shawn went to his next class, stupefied and defeated again by a genius.

Shawn Baron retreated for a while in order to challenge *'Brains'* at another time. The question was how Brains could solve that problem so quickly.

# CHAPTER 5

# Down Town

Starting around 1975 and ending around 1980, came a new dance craze: ***Disco Dancing***.

Many teens and young adults hooked up together to go to the '***Disco***' and groove to the music, while being bathed in multi-coloured rotating lights. The combination of lights (*reflected from a rotating disco ball, made of small square mirrors*) and the beat of the music helped encourage the dancers to gyrate their hips, while using fancy arm and footwork.

By now, Noah was growing into a tall and distinguished youth. He was starting to develop a well-chiselled face and masculine figures, which made a few female heads, turn. Since it had been over five weeks that he turned fourteen, Noah met the love of his life.

Hanging out with a few of his friends and celebrating the passing of his grade twelve exams, Noah was struck by Cupid's arrow when he spied the most beautiful foxy lady in the world. He caught sight of her just after he got a medium soft drink from an island vender. She astounded him.

She too was fourteen years old with large brown eyes, high cheekbones, slender nose and full puffy lips. Being in grade ten, she had shoulder length Mahogany hair, long slender legs and slim curvy figure, which captured Noah's attention. She was a semblance of a female model that walked with style and gracefulness, which definitely stole his heart. Even though she wore pale jeans and a winter coat over a yellow blouse, Noah knew beauty when he saw it. He had to talk to her.

He excused himself and leaving his friends behind, Noah approached this captivating fem-fatale, cautiously, to introduce himself.

The young woman was examining some clothes displayed in a clothing store window. She was trying to visualize herself in one of the dresses or dress suits when …

"I think that would look lovely on you," stated Noah with a grin.

Startled out of her visualization, she stared at Noah with enlarged eyes of fear, without saying a word.

"Forgive me," continued Noah, "I didn't mean to startle you. I just wanted to introduce myself. My name is Noah. Noah Body. What is your name?"

Speaking quietly and blushing due to her shyness, she said, "Crystal! " Still speaking with a little fear and scanning the mall around her, she continued, "*Crystal Parsons*."

"Wait a moment! Are you related to *Carey Thomas Parsons*?"

"Yes! He's my father," stated Crystal coldly.

Carey Thomas Parsons was the new local automotive mechanic in town. He had purchased the local garage and called it '**Carey's Auto Repairs**'. This man had a vast knowledge of automobiles and their parts. Whether it was a car, truck, tractor, train, plane, motorbike or tank, Carey was the man to go to for help. He was an honest, clean and industrious worker. His work place had to meet his high standards of cleanliness. Every tool in his shop had its own marked location and needed to return at the end of each day in those marked designations. He never bilked the public out of their hard-earned money by deliberately damaging automotive parts on someone's vehicle, so he could milk them for more cash.

When he moved his family from Colorado in June, he made a small fortune from his enterprising mechanical shop there. Now he was starting over again in a smaller community and providing his specialty services there. Only one thing he did classify as a drawback. Mr. Parsons had a drinking problem. If a person had gotten to know him better, it was understandable why his drinking problem began.

Two years before moving, a drunken driver smashed into his wife's small car, killing her instantly. Carey loved his wife and never harmed her. After her death, he felt lost without her support and turned to the same poison that killed his wife. When he got drunk, he became a ruthless and violent man. This dark side of his reputation followed him everywhere he went. In order to start fresh again, Mr. Parsons needed to sell his business, relocate and begin anew (*this included cutting out alcohol altogether, not an easy thing for him to do*).

This made it hard on Crystal. There were the odd times her father would beat her if her marks were below a '**B**' level. She would walk around with a turtleneck sweater on, even on hot summer days, trying to hide the black and blue marks she received. She also had to prepare meals, wash dishes and do the laundry since her mother's death, besides doing any homework and other school assignments that needed completion. Both father and daughter suffered together through their loss. A hope for a fresh start aided them both to get back on track with their lives.

"If my father saw you talking to me, he'd kill you right where you stand," stated Crystal coldly.

Not fizzed by her cold warning, Noah quietly drank his drink and pondered as to what to say next. That is when Crystal spoke again.

"Wait a minute!" squinting her brown eyes, "Aren't you that genius kid who outsmarted Shawn Baron a few weeks ago? Boy, to stand up to that bully, must have taken plenty of guts. Weren't you afraid?"

"Yes, it was a difficult challenge. No, I was not afraid. I already knew that a jock like him was unable to come up with the answers to my questions. Remember, Shawn's focus on life is to be the best in sports. There is not much call for the use of complicated mathematical equations in football or hockey. Because of that incident and my love of games, my friends like to refer to me as 'The Game Master' or 'GM' for short."

"WOW! That's a cool name," looking down before she continued, "I'd wished I had a cool nickname." Relaxing and allowing her guard down a little, Crystal felt comfortable being around GM. Then she felt slightly embarrassed about being cold to the neatest and brainiest boy in school. Yet, she still did not want to let her guard down completely.

"It is truly an honour to meet you Crystal," Noah stated. "How's about a name like …" thinking for a moment, Noah came up with a nickname for her "…*Prairie Lily*."

Crystal loved the nickname he gave her. However, Noah's next action made her blush several more shades of red.

Then Noah took one of her hands in his and quickly bent over, kissed it. Standing upright again he continued, "I also wanted to welcome you to Red Bluff, California and to the Red Bluff Regional High School."

She never had another school student before address her in such an unusual manner. Before removing her hand rapidly and placing it back into her coat pocket, she enjoyed this brief moment of attention and smiled. It was the first time she felt very comfortable around Noah and she was now willing to let down her guard, in his presence.

Noah clued in on her reaction and said, "Until we meet again… Prairie Lily?"

Smiling now for the first time this semester, Crystal said, "Yes. I'd like that very much … GM."

She waved goodbye to Noah as he slipped through the crowded mall. It was the first time a boy showed any interest in her. However, her fear was not without cause. In several seconds, her ruthless father's reflection appeared in the store window and demanded to know what was going on. Crystal explained in a terrified voice and a rapid-fire answer, that it was a fellow student from her school. She was preparing herself for the blow that was going to come because she talked to someone of the opposite sex. Instead, her father just stared at GM's backside when he rejoined his friends. Making a disgusted face and grunting his displeasure, Carey mumbled under his breath, "Let's go home Cupcake!"

Following her father, Crystal felt she was going to get it later that evening. When they entered the family car, both of them remained silent for the trip home from the mall.

Crystal had already finished the supper dishes and put the leftovers into the fridge.

She next tackled her math homework, when the pelting sound against the widow indicated the rain shower to come. For a brief moment, the sound distracted her concentration and the rhythmic beating of the raindrops hitting the glass pane sent her mind wandering. For some reason Crystal was back in the previous town they lived in and it too was a rainy night when...

*A knock came to her bedroom door. Stiffening upright, Crystal knew she was in for it. With a trembling voice, she said, "Come in!" It was her father. Thinking of the worst-case scenario possible was about to happen, she tensed and waited to see what he would do.*

*Carey was very much a sober man. He was trying harder than ever not to break his oath to his daughter about stopping his drinking problem. This was not easy for him. In time, Mr. Parsons began to let go of his pent up anger and depression over the loss of his wife. This required that he attempt to give up his dominating attitude over his daughter. She was slowly blossoming into a youthful woman and would soon leave the family nest. His over-protectiveness towards her inexperience about life and helping her to understand his fatherly feelings toward her needed expression.*

"Umm … Do you have a moment, Cupcake?" queried Carey. "Yes father … I do! Come in."

"Sorry to interrupt you while you're doing your homework. I just needed to share a concern I have with you."

"It's alright Dad. I was on my last mathematical question when you knocked," she closed her books. "What did you want to see me about?"

He came over to her bed and sat down beside her. Taking her hands into his and looking Crystal straight in the eyes, Carey said, "Honey. I don't think that I'm a very good father to you …"

"But dad, you've always been there for …" Crystal began to interrupt.

"I know Cupcake! I know. However, until we move, I will be a violent and horrible father to you. I got drunk and hurt you physically and emotionally in a way that no father should ever do to his daughter." He paused, "I want to apologize for my ugly behaviour these past two years. It was uncalled for and very wrong on my part. I used your mother's death as an excuse not to be responsible for my own actions and not to make any effort to move forward in my life, despite her loss. I turned to the same bottle of venom that contributed to your mother's death. I was wrong, totally in the wrong. And I hope you can find it in your heart to forgive your old man for his callus demeanour towards you," tears started to stream down his face.

"Yes father. Oh yes I can forgive you," cried Crystal as she reached up to hug her father. She could tell this was not easy for him to do. Only a true loving man would admit his errors and be willing to make amends.

*"I'm so sorry Cupcake," he reached up and hugged his daughter, "I'm so sorry to hurt my precious one." Now the tears flowed from both of them and they both continued to hold each other for a minute. Carey continued to apologize and Crystal kept reassuring him of her forgiveness.*

*When they did let each other go and sit back. They wiped their eyes before Carey continued,*

*"That really means a lot to me Cupcake. Thank you." He bent over and kissed his daughter on the forehead. "I am also working on a promise to avoid booze at any cost. Nevertheless, I cannot do it alone. Would you be willing to assist me through this troublesome time? I need your help to survive through this mourning process together."*

*"Yes father. I'm willing to assist you in any way I can," smiled Crystal as she gave her father another reassuring hug.*

*"Good! Good," Carey got up to leave. "I better let you finish your homework. Thank you for having this talk with me Cupcake. I just needed to get some things off of my chest which had been bothering me these last two years."*

*"That's ok - Dad. I'm always here if you need..."*

...A knocking sound on her bedroom door snapped Crystal out of her daydreaming. Startled back to reality, Crystal knew it was her father coming to talk to her about something of importance. With a trembling voice, she said, "Come in!" Thinking back to the earlier events at the mall, Crystal figured she was in deep trouble, for talking to that boy from school. This caused her muscles to tense up.

Carey leaned in holding onto Crystal's bedroom door. "Sorry to interrupt you while you're doing your homework

Cupcake. I was just going to go to bed early tonight since I have a big repair job tomorrow morning and I thought I would check with you to see if you needed any help with your homework."

"Thank you for asking dad, but I'm almost done."

"OK then. I will let you finish up. Goodnight, Cupcake!"

Relaxing Crystal said, "Goodnight, Papa!"

As Carey was about to close the bedroom door, he stopped and then reopened the door. "You made a wonderful supper this evening Cupcake. How's about I make a Barbeque Steak supper Saturday night? I'll even do the dishes!"

Giggling for a moment, Crystal said, "That'd be wonderful Dad."

Then like an afterthought, "By the way, the boy you talked to earlier today at the mall, did he happen to mention his name to you?"

Crystal's fear returned, trembling at the thought she was in deep shit, "Yes," she squeezed out, "his name ... his name was Noah! That's right, his name was Noah Body."

Thinking for a moment and then laughing aloud before closing the bedroom door, he said, "What an unusual name." Pausing for a moment, Carey asked, "Why don't you invite this ... Noah and his parents over to our Barbeque?"

Breathing a sigh of relief, Crystal replied, "Ok Papa! I'll ask them over."

"That's wonderful sweet heart! Well, goodnight Cupcake."

"Goodnight, Papa!"

= = =

Time can be an allusive but active friend or foe. One moment, a person seems to be accomplishing many items on a list they have and getting these tasks done rapidly, even before the day ends. On other occasions, a person never seems to get more than one or two items done on their list; moving as with lead feet and concrete brains; leaving the unfinished work load for the next day. As crazy as this illusion may seem, time has a way of also healing wounds and bridging gaps between people. Although active and allusive, time is always running in a steady stream forward, leaving humans behind in its wake or forever makes people try to catch up.

In the case of Noah and Crystal, time was an ally for the both of them during this occasion. Noah accepted the loss of his father, while Crystal adjusted to her father's changed positive personality. Although they did not want to it known they were lovers, both parties did things together very discreetly and quietly in the beginning similar to what Noah's parents did in their youth.

One Saturday afternoon, Noah asked Crystal if she would like to join him and his friends at the local Disco. She accepted his invitation and met him there. Many of their classmates were already having a fun time on the dance floor. Being teenagers and awkward on their feet, both dancers finally got the hang of dancing to the beat. After dancing for approximately two hours, they cooled off every now and then, with refreshments before leaving for home.

The Disco was not the only place these two are together. On other occasions, they went to movies or they just hung out at the *Franklin Mall* down town. On a few occasional weekends, Crystal did odd jobs for her father. As for GM, he would go out with his friends doing other fun activities or check up on his stock market challenge.

Both of these individuals did not mind being apart from one another. Quiet times were for either studying for exams or reflecting on good times they had together. Both respected each other's boundaries and never crossed over these lines of limitations. Like two respectable and morally upright individuals, neither Crystal nor Noah allowed room for peer pressure to force them to do anything against their wills. Dignity, respect and open communication were the order of the day.

One day an announcement came over the school P.A. System. It stated that any students who wanted to join in the production of the play - *Pygmalion* - could join in a drama class after school. Although neither of them ever acted before, Noah and Crystal wanted to try out the new avenue offered. Joining in this same drama class were other students. The grade eleven students were *Jay Cochran*, *Elizabeth Ceiling* and *Nelson Cocoa*. From the grade ten students were *George White Feather*, *Shane Hunter*, *Sylvia Winch*, *Jade Soon* and 6 others.

As time went by, most of the students enjoyed role-playing on stage. Like a game in itself, the play mimicked life and easily acted out with great finesse. The energy and emotions from the students provided the realism to the story lines and the characters they portrayed. As a result, the play was a great success for the school and students. After graduating from school, most of these students continued to do stage productions in the old brick *Red Bluff Theatre*, on Main Street.

Yet a problem existed in the early stages of the school production. Shane and Sylvia hardly showed up for their rehearsals and dropped out of their roles. These two had their interests and eyesight elsewhere.

Shane was a stocky; fifteen year old who stood five foot six inches, with dark, curly hair and piercing blue-green eyes. He had a well-tuned athletic body for his height, Italian type facial features and a sexual predatory charisma that some females could not resist. He used his overactive sexual prowess and charm to get in bed with any female he met. Then after two weeks or so with the same girl, he would demonstrate his true intellect by dumping that female for another one. In the production of the school play, he attracted the attention of the sleazy Sylvia.

For a brunette, fifteen years old Sylvia turned out to be a sexual tramp to her neighbours. She stood five feet nine inches tall with light brown eyes. She had a slim female hourglass figure and large sensuous lips. Her reputation as a sexual fiend or hooker would not easily leave her. Sylvia enjoyed sexual intercourse since the age of fourteen and could not get enough from the aphrodisiac high. Most of her male partners would lose their momentum after a couple of hours with her. Sylvia on the other hand could go on and on and on, like the energizer bunny.

Despite this flaw in her character, she also had the ability to mastermind her way through problems or business possibilities like raising money for school outings or create various school activities for her fellow students, so they could take a break from secular learning. She was a bright student, but very deadly to tango with.

Because of her rotten reputation and scheming mind, Noah got into a predicament with this wench of trashiness. The clashes of brilliant minds were about to begin and lasted almost twenty years.

# CHAPTER 6

# What Evil Schemes
# Hath Thou Rot

The stock market seemed to be in a stalemated position for the last thirteen months until a hint of the starting upward trend began to show. It was unknown whether Noah's instincts kicked in or not, but he was able to sell his first shares and almost doubled his money from the original $950.00. Without taking the funds out, he decided to reinvest them into other stocks. Within a week, he had increased his portfolio by almost an additional 4.8%. Still not giving up and feeling he was successful, Noah reinvested his moneys again into some long-term stocks, penny stocks, bonds and gold bullion. His timing could never have been better.

Graduating from high school about two years earlier than normal, Noah continued to play the stock market as a challenging game. During his final year in high school, his principal suggested he try the stock markets for real. Noah was doing that. He adapted the rules from the board game, Monopoly and applied them (*along with the **Elliott Wave***

*Theory*[4]) to the stock markets. Then he waited for the big surge upwards to come.

In late spring of 1979, the stock market began its aggressive Bull Run upwards and Noah made vast profits from his buying and selling of various stocks and bonds in rapid surges. Within four months, he was worth $750,980.

In another three months, he was close to $2.95 Million. Noah was doing exceptionally well and he was not going to give up.

Two months later Noah hit a jackpot of just over $10 Million. This added to his portfolio. Yet the stock market at times became like a drug to him. He could not get enough of the opium-like effect it gave him. He could not have the money until he turned eighteen.

This fifteen year olds portrait was on the cover of Time Magazine and Business Newsweek for being the youngest Multi-Millionaire. As for Noah, he continued to enjoy the problem of outguessing the stocks momentum and continued to turn over vast profits. It seemed every stock or bond he chose made him even more money than the previous times.

The publicity from the Time Magazine about Noah's wealth attracted the attention of scheming Sylvia. She had plans for his money, which excluded Noah from the picture. Yet she could not do it alone, she needed an accomplice or two. *Who could help me?*

Thinking carefully, a two part complex plan brewed within her mind. She needed at least two willing, if not, dumb males

---

[4]    For some information on this topic, please go to Appendix "D".

to accomplish her task. Who to get to do her dirty work was the main question! Shawn Baron was the first one that came to mind. '*Yes, Shawn will do nicely. He'll want revenge since the math stunt Noah did to him two years before.*' Tomorrow she would enlist this burly bully leader and some of the *Hacksaw Barons* to her cause.

It could never have happened to the kindest of people. One rainy spring weekend while Noah was at the evening movie with his friend Jay, Crystal went to the **Red Cliff Public Library**, on 2nd Street, seeking out extra information about the country China for her Monday school paper. While continuing her research, Crystal had no idea that two pairs of eyes were watching her from the second story shelf units.

"There's his sweetheart. If you want to destroy his life, she is the one you need to target and convince that you're the only one for her," declared Sylvia in a low whispered tone.

"I don't know," whispered Shawn, "This will not be easy to pull off on my own." Looking away from the potential prey, staring into Sylvia's eyes, he continued, "The only person I know who can mimic Noah's voice would be … Roger. Otherwise, it will fail. "

"Then get going and prepare!"

"When," he questioned.

"Tonight, you idiot! This would be the perfect evening to do it when she heads home," Sylvia and Shawn looked back at their foe. "If I'm not mistaken, she will lose track of the time. Realizing how late in the night it will be, she will try cutting through **Central Park** to get home faster. Just make sure that the Central Park lights are not working except for one. Then all will go according to my plans."

"You better be right," Shawn continued to whisper. "We, the Hacksaw Barons, are taking quite a risk if this doesn't work."

Scowling and staring at Shawn, Sylvia stated, "If you guys follow my plans to the letter, it will work! Now, go get ready!"

Shawn quietly slipped out of the library, unnoticed by Crystal as he left.

Sylvia glared back at Crystal, "You will go away my dear precious. Yes, you will be gone forever out of Noah's life and I'll control that brainless twit's money."

After two minutes, Sylvia also slipped out of the library.

Not realizing how late she was in the library, Crystal heard the final closing call five minutes to 9 pm. Collecting her research papers and holding them close to her chest, Crystal headed for home.

After crossing from 2nd Street to 1st Street, Prairie Lily decided to cross through *Central Park* to reach her home on Maple Avenue. After ten-minutes of walking, she would be home, unharmed.

Red Cliff's Central Park was a simple rectangular design. In the middle of the park, a donut shaped water fountain surrounding a four-headed street lamp, with a circular stone picnic table and benches around the lamp base. The park's metal mesh fence surrounded the exterior border of the park. At the corners of the fence were four openings and a meandering sidewalk that created an oblong x shape toward the centre of the park. The well-manicured Park lawns and flower gardens continued through the summer months. During the winter months, various ice sculptures and snow hills provided for family outdoor fun. Red Cliff Counsel was happy to have this acre of land for public usage.

Six minutes into her walk toward the centre of the park, Crystal's senses told her that danger was lurking in the darkness ahead. Stopping to take a quick look around her, she saw nothing out of the ordinary, not even the two grey, non-moving figures behind a tree caught her attention. The streetlights in the centre of the park looked burned out, with the exception of one that was still shining. With only one light on, the park seemed to create mysterious and eerie shadows. As for the other three lights, no one could tell at night that they were deliberately smashed to create the darkness.

Despite this nerve racking position, Crystal's senses kept telling her there was danger nearby.

*Something feels out of place!*

Crystal's internal voice dictated that speed was of the essence. *The atmosphere feels wrong. I just want to run home, now,* Crystal thought. She picked up her pace and headed for the west corner gate.

As she made a beeline through the grass of Central Park to the west gate, Prairie Lily did not expect the attack that came from behind her.

Two masked figures knocked her down onto the manicured lawn. Her books and research papers flew from her hands and landed ten feet away. Crystal struggled with her two strong assailants, making every effort to gain the upper hand and freedom. It was to no avail, her assailants continued to fight with her, ripping some of her clothes and slapping her now and then.

Then one assailant asked the other, "What will we do next?"

The other assailant in Noah's voice stated flatly, "We'll rape her and then kill her!"

Upon hearing, what she thought was Noah's voice; Crystal stared in jolted disbelief at the voice behind the mask.

"Let's do it," Noah's voice answered. Laughter broke out between the two male assailants.

"No! Get off me! GET OFF OF ME," yelled Crystal, trying desperately to get these two freaks off her person. She then remembered a school course that taught the girls to scream an important word aloud and was better than yelling help. "Fire, Fire, **FIRE!**" she hoped these words would do the trick. Her screams did assist her indeed that frightful evening!

It was at the point that the two assailants began ripping away Crystal's undergarments, blouse and skirt while fondling her exposed breasts. Still struggling with her assailants, a loud deep masculine voice yelled out from behind the fence line, **"GET YOUR FRIGGING HANDS OFF OF HER - YOU BASTARDS!"** It was Shawn Baron and he charged in the direction of the two masked individuals.

Interrupted by the intruder during their fun, the assailants let go of their prize and split the scene while Shawn continued in hot pursuit. He chased them out of the park, but they were too fast for him and disappeared out of sight.

For the first time, Crystal was glad that Shawn happened to be in the area. Nevertheless, she curled up into a foetal position crying, suffering from trauma and embarrassment of her terrible appearance. *How could Noah do such a thing to me? I thought we respected each other.*

Shawn jogged back to help the victim.

She tried to stand up but found it hard too; the attack took a lot of energy from her body and she collapsed back to the ground. While trying to help her up a second time, Shawn noticed the bruises began to show and cut marks that bled.

"Are you ok, Crystal?" asked the concerned Shawn.

"I'm just a little dizzy and startled," replied Crystal, trying hard to cover up any of her nakedness from Shawn's eyes.

"Allow me to help you up. Do you know who attacked you?" queried Shawn. He looked around to see if the assailants would return, while he assisted Crystal.

"One of them sounded exactly like Noah. I'd assumed the other one was either Jay or Nelson!"

"They'll pay dearly for this!" Shawn stated flatly. "May I walk you to your house?"

"Yes, please do," Crystal, stated. Stopping for a moment and looking around her, "My research! Where's my research gone?" She looked all around the grassing lawn.

"I see them. You wait here, I'll get them for you," replied Shawn. Walking ten feet away from the scene of the crime, Shawn picked up every piece of paper and books he could find before the evening breeze blew them away. Upon returning to Crystal, he found her crying again uncontrollably and holding up pieces of her torn blouse and broken bra strap.

Without saying a word, he removed his school jacket and wrapped it around her shoulders. Then he slowly gave her a hug and patted her on the back, "There! There! You're all right now. Let me walk you home, precious." After letting her go, he offered his arm to her. Hesitant at first and still shaking from the trauma she had gone through, Crystal relented and put her arm through Shawn's arm, tightly hugging it. Slowly they both walked quietly to her house on #22 Maple Avenue and called the police.

When the planned assault took place in the park, GM and Jay were enjoying the movie they attended. The movie's ten-minute delay and the time they left the show, it was close to 9:30 pm. Neither Jay nor Noah knew anything about the attack on Prairie Lily until both boys arrived at Noah's home twenty minutes later.

Carey Parsons was on the phone to Connie Body and furious about what had happened to his daughter. His phone call made accusations that Noah and a friend attempted to rape his daughter. He also informed Connie that if Shawn Baron had not been walking home at the time, his daughter would be dead.

Connie was in a traumatized state and couldn't believe that her son was involved in such a situation. Her son told her that he was going to the movies with his friend Jay, but Mr. Parsons wouldn't listen. He got the police involved and laid charges against both boys. As for her son Noah, dating Crystal, that was to end immediately.

After the phone call, both Noah and Jay explained that they didn't commit the horrifying crime that Prairie Lily claimed happened to her. Both of them produced the movie ticket stubs that proved they were where they claimed to be.

When the police arrived, the boys explained the exact same story to the officers and showed them the same ticket stubs. Not only did they claim to be at the theatre that night, but also, they were able to relate various movie scenes and the actors that played in the show. The other point was very clear, the Theatre was on the other side of town and it would have taken the boys twenty-seven minutes to get to Central Park. After all said and done, the police officer informed Noah to no longer to have any dealings with Carey's daughter, Crystal. If Noah was on or caught, anywhere near their property, he would go to jail and court proceedings would take place.

Noah and Jay couldn't believe their ears. The shock waves that trembled through Noah's body made his heart sink to an all-time low. With great reluctance, Noah finally agreed with the two officers, just before they left that he would not go anywhere near the Parsons house.

That night, the poor lad couldn't sleep very well. He knew this was a false accusation, but how could he prove it?

That Sunday morning, Noah resembled something a ten-ton truck had run over. Blood shot eyes; depressed expression and sleepy appearance greeted his mother that morning at breakfast. Connie could tell her son had a hard night trying to sleep and that he was possibly so shook up that he might have been crying. She tried to reassure her son to be strong and that other fish were in the sea to scoop up. She also indicated that the truth would come out and this incident would blow over. Yet Noah had never been so emotionally down before. He hardly ate a thing for breakfast. All he could think of was going to jail and his mom left all alone.

Jay came over to cheer up Noah. Although he was with Noah the night before and he knew the truth about that evening, it was to no avail he tried to cheer up his friend. Noah just kept moping, not eating and refusing to accept her false story. After some conversation, Noah thought maybe he could talk to her at school. Jay warned him of the possible consequences if Carey Parsons found out. However, GM finally saw a possible light at the end of the rainbow. By pinning her down after classes, he could ask her what really went on that evening. Little did Noah realize was that his hopes would be dashed.

When Monday morning rolled around, Noah got up early to see if he could catch Crystal before she entered the school grounds. He waited for twenty minutes hiding in the only clump of trees and bushes on the corner of the schoolyard. Suddenly he spotted Shawn standing at the entrance of the school. *What are you doing here?*

It was at that moment that Carey Parsons drove his car up to the school entrance. Shawn made his way over to the driver's side and started talking to Mr. Parsons. *What are you up too?* asked Noah. *Why are you talking to Mr. Parsons? I thought Mr. Parson didn't allow scum near his daughter!*

After a couple of minutes, Shawn walked around to the passenger side and opened the door, like a gentleman, for Crystal. As Prairie Lily left the car, Shawn then offered to take her books for her and walk her to her locker. Smiling again, Crystal accepted his invitation. When they started to walk, Shawn offered his strong arm for her to take a hold of and she gladly accepted this offering as well. Both of them walked arm in arm into the school with Carey's approval.

Noah couldn't handle this injustice and his temperature rose. *That's my girlfriend, not yours!* He had to act fast! Therefore, he left from his hiding place and went to catch Crystal in order to straighten things out.

Mr. Parsons was glad Shawn was there to protect and stay close by his daughter because of this fiendish incident two nights before. As he started his car to drive away, he spotted Noah walking thirty feet away from the paved entrance of the high school. His murderous rage flared to life and he gunned his car engine with the intent to run down the young sexual pervert.

"You bloody sexual predator! How dare you touch my daughter! In addition, how dare you show your face around here! You're going to pay for what you did to my precious girl," declared Carey. He sped off straight at GM. He was a little too slow at catching the kid; the boy was fast and agile.

Noah saw the car coming with other students dashing out of the way. He spun around quickly and headed across the street for safety.

Mr. Parson was gaining on Noah when the boy pulled a fast one. At the last possible second, Noah dodged right and ducked down a back alley.

Slamming on his brakes, Carey almost hit someone's garage, but wiped out their garbage cans instead. Cussing under his breath, he redirecting his car to head downs the back alley after the boy. Carey had lost some time by falling behind the target. At least this set back would not be for long!

Noah needed to escape from the manic motorist. As Mr. Parsons backed his car up to head down the back alley, Noah found an open gate and dove into the back yard. He closed the gate quickly and dropped down behind the fence. Breathing heavily he waited for an opportunity to make his next move.

Mr. Parsons drove down the alley but he lost sight of Noah. He drove slowly and examined each yard he drove past. "Where is that fiend? Come out; come out where ever you are! I want to drive over you – you sexual pervert! You think you can get away with hurting my precious girl!"

When the coast was clear Noah cut through the backyard, he was hiding in. Shaking from fear and anxiety, GM fled in the opposite direction of the car. Although it wasn't easy, he finally made his get away by ducking around various alleys and streets, until he made it home.

Later that morning, Noah told his mother what had happened. With the police involved a second time, GM was given a final warning to stay away from the Parsons. As for Mr. Parson, he too had a warning given to him to stop pursuing people with his vehicle and running them over.

Connie made her *Nobby* vow that he would never go near the high school again, for any reason. This incident made Noah go into a deep depression, because he had lost the only person he wanted to marry.

*How could this happen? I'm innocent! I didn't hurt Prairie Lily! I was no way near her at the time. Jay could vouch for me! He was with me when we went to the movie theatre together.*

After that day, Noah stayed out of sight.

"I love it when a plan comes together," stated Sylvia. "Now for the second phase of my plan..." Every chance she got, Sylvia took great care to make sure all the girls in school knew about the attempted sexual assault on Crystal by Noah and the heroic efforts of Shawn to thwart the attack.

Shawn loved all the attention he was getting from all the other females. He went out of his way to make the girls swoon over his muscular physique and gloated in all the attention he was receiving.

Prairie Lily gained a support group with the other girls, who fought against sexual violence. All of the girls rallied around her and protected her from any bullies.

Noah's name became mud throughout the school and community. Every time he showed his face at the mall or at the movies, the other girls from the high school ignored him or hurled insults or food at him. Their parents would scorn Noah and even chased him out of many businesses. There were only four locations Noah was restricted to, the Town Library, the Red Bluff Theatre, his home or the Stock Market Exchange.

Sylvia Winch's scheme succeeded beyond her wildest dreams. From a distance, she observed Noah hiding across the street and watched his love loss. Noah's defeated expressions and sagging body language gave Sylvia great ecstasy. Her plan was to separate Crystal from Noah and it worked.

To add more salt to Noah's wounds, Sylvia went as far as to inform Shawn of Noah's reactions. Every time Noah saw Shawn and Crystal cuddling together, it would lacerate Noah's heart apart. Shawn was thrilled at hearing how much pain he was inflicting on Noah, a person who should have done his homework for him two years before. Since Shawn had to repeat his last semester because of poor marks, for him this was payback time, in a big way!

To add to GM's depression, Shawn went as far as to send threatening notes and leaving them on the porch bench at Noah's home. Shawn concealed his rotten deed. Each word selected came from various newspaper and magazine articles. In a cut-and-paste style, Shawn never told Sylvia about bullying Noah in this manner.

Every now and then Noah would spy on Crystal from across the street, opposite the school. He observed Shawn kissing his former Prairie Lily, walking hand and hand or holding her in a tight romantic embrace. This alliance with one of his enemies finally broke Noah's heart. With tears in his hazel eyes, Noah quit pursuing his former love after three weeks. It was hard for him to believe and to take the punishment for losing big time to this school bully.

"Goodbye Forever … Prairie Lily!" he said through his tears.

Now, only time could heal such a wounded heart.

= = =

In order to compensate for his depression and severe loss during this period, Noah concentrated his energy on his stock market gambit. It was during this time that he increased his portfolio well over $77.7 million within nine months.

To assist him to go forward at this same time, a few of his friends rallied around him and encouraged him to join their theatrical enterprise - *The Red Bluff Players*. If Noah got used to working on stage and playing the role of another person, he could enjoy life again - seeing it through the eyes of a character in the play. This he gladly accepted.

After they put on one stage production, Noah still felt the need to leave the area for a while. He found it difficult to live in the same area as his ex-sweetheart and her bully boyfriend; it was time to move on. He didn't say a word to any of his friends about the six threatening notes he had received over the last seven weeks, each worse than the last ones. He had to escape the madness!

When he turned eighteen, Noah bought himself a small car and drove off into the sunset to clear his head. He needed to find a new place to live and ended up on the west side of the state of *Idaho* in *Custard County*.

At first, it was hard for Connie to understand why her youngest had to run away. Then she discovered why her son left so quickly, she found the threatening letters on top of her son's dresser, two days after he left town. If her youngest one had to flee from these death threats, neither she nor any family members would divulge Noah's whereabouts.

In the meantime, Connie took these letters and made copies of them all. Then she took the originals over to the same officers who worked on the attempted rape case. They both informed Connie that they would take care of the matter. It became eventually obvious that the police did nothing about the letters, because Connie never heard from those officers again!

The first part of Sylvia's plan was simple, all Shawn had to do was steal away Noah's love life and he would crumble. With this part of the task accomplished, she went on to the second phase of the plan: destroyed Noah's name and reputation with other female students. This would eliminate any competition for his money and would make Noah more vulnerable for the picking. To succeed in this task, Sylvia would eventually have this young man under her domination. Yes, he would fall into her arms with great ease and obey her every whim.

It was now time to implement the final phase of her scheme into action.

*Now whom could I get to assist me at this task? Which stooge could I use to employ final part of my plans?*

Taking a moment to ponder out the answer, Sylvia made a snapping sound of her fingers, *Of course - Shane Hunter! He'll do nicely*, she thought.

*All one has to do is work out the details. Mastermind, you've out done yourself again*, she mused. *Now I must see this job through.*

One little hitch wrecked her plans for the time being. Noah had disappeared from the area and none of his family or his friends knew his locale. If they did know, not one word slipped out.

"You won't disappear from me that easily! Not for long!" declared the predator. "I'll find you sooner or later."

= = =

Fleeing from Red Cliff California and wandering around the country, Noah explored every location he came across. Two months had elapsed before he arrived in the state of Idaho.

The county of Custard, on the mid-western side of Idaho, was very welcoming location for Noah. He liked the mountainous terrain with the odd jutting plateaus of earth and rugged peaked mountains. On the tops of these hilly mountain peaks, the farmers at times grew crops at angles of approximately 35 to 60 degrees and had ways of harvesting those same fields without tumbling down the hillside. The toes of land on some mountains added to the landscape and created some beautiful vantage points, to view the valley areas below.

When the wild flowers bloomed in the springtime, vast meadows untouched by human hands seemed to appear overnight. Colours waved in the wind from everywhere! Flowers of every shape, style and colour covered the landmass, added to the greenery around it. Yes, Idaho was a gorgeous state in the spring.

Noah just loved the area and this was where he found sixty acres of land for sale.

The **Seltzer Family** couple that owned the **Seltzer Ranch** were getting older and could no longer handle the maintenance of the locale. Neither their children nor their grandchildren wanted the spread anymore. Their eldest son insisted that his parents sell it and move in with his family in Arizona. Although these two didn't really want to sell their precious horse range, their aging bodies demanded that they should consider the possibility of doing so. Therefore, they put it up for sale.

Noah couldn't resist buying it on the spot. He offered to pay the Seltzer's almost twice their asking price - $240,000. Mind-blown at first by his offer, they politely removed themselves for a private discussion about GM's terms. Returning five minutes later, they concluded that they couldn't refuse Noah's offer! They all headed down to the local bank in the town of Custard in order to fill out the bill of sale and transfer the deed of the ranch to GM. Noah paid the Seltzer's with a certified bank draft. After shaking hands, the Seltzers left town for their son's home in Arizona.

The ranch was located just off highway #113; on a half circular plateau six miles in circumference. It rose above the lower valley floor by approximately two thousand feet. The former occupants planted half of the trees growing around this ranch – mostly pine trees, with a few large cedars mixed in.

The ranch house was small and falling apart in different places. Paint had peeled away and the roof leaked profusely during the rainy season. GM saw the need for a new ranch house to replace the old one and he was going to expand the foundation of the home with a new larger layout.

Just off to the left of the house was the barn, containing the horse stables. This was another disaster waiting to happen. Its roof was now a real dangerous swayback with huge cracks running along the support beams and studs. The lower half of the barn leaned left while the roof leaned right. This gave the appearance that the barn would collapse at any moment onto itself even if a person happened to sneeze that direction.

Some of the fencing and corrals needed lumber replacements badly. Several pieces of wood were broken and rotted away to dust. One piece of solid wood had carpenter ants chewing tunnels through it and rendering the wood weak like sponge toffee. Changes needed to take place!

Even an old outhouse stood off to the right of the house, in the bushes. Its age had caused the building to lean dangerously on its right side and slightly backwards. Only a couple of boards seemed to desperately hold the building upright, while the rest were either pulled out of place or broken over time, as if a heavy weight hit the boards. All the buildings definitely have to go!

Seven miles away from the ranch, a dirt road made several twists and turns through patches of forest to eventually end at a large parking spot overlooking the *Sunshine Valley*. Here a gravelled parking lot cut into the side of a hill, later known as *Seven Mile Hill*. Beside the lot, overlooking the hill's edge was a large split open boulder.

The boulder had a giant crack running through the middle of it, along with a gravelled pathway running through that crevasse. From certain viewpoints, the boulder obscured this trail leading down the middle of the rock. If a person found the trail, they would head down the hill through a thick forest fifty feet below. This clump of forest opened into a large hector-sized meadow of wild flowers.

The Valley's beauty from this vantage point seemed to stretch for miles, except for the patches of forest obscuring some viewpoints around the cliff's edge and the boulder.

Noah fell more and more in love with his purchase. The entire ranch needed a complete overhaul and some modernizing to finish off the new appearance of the place. He felt the old-fashioned rustic look of the present buildings were uncoordinated with the times.

Therefore, GM hired a draftsman to design the various rooms he wanted on the house floor plans, servant's quarters and the new barn (*with stables*).

Next, he hired a local contractor to build the new buildings according to the new drafting plans. Later he hired a local interior decorator to decorate the interior of the house and servant's quarters.

One room in the ranch house floor plans asked for was a larger living room space, 15 feet by 20 feet, with the old-fashioned stone fireplace mounted on one wall. Trying hard to use local materials, Noah used the colourful local stones to add to the beauty and function of the fireplace. A shelf positioned above the stonework to place little nick-knacks on and added to the beauty of the room. Just above the shelf was a blank wall to hang a large picture, if a person wanted to, above the fireplace.

The plans also included a step built around the entire living room area. When a person stepped down the one-step, they were standing in a sunken living room floor. In case of a future accident were a person might be in a wheelchair. Noah had the foresight to add three small ramps built onto the stepped floor one leading into the kitchen area, another one leading to the hallway opposite the patio doors and the last leading to a set of patio doors on the south side of the living room. The entire carpeted room was in a light blue and grey patterned rug.

The sliding patio doors emptied out into a roofed balcony ten feet by twelve. Inside the wooden balcony was a wall containing benches built onto the walls. In one corner was a pair of swinging saloon doors that swung open onto the cobble-stoned garden beyond. The middle of the balcony was a spot for a propane barbeque oven and a chimneystack built into the middle of the roof to act as a ventilation unit.

Attached to the living room, opposite the fireplace and on the east side of the building, was a huge open archway that connected the quarter pie shaped dining room and kitchen. The wooden floors added to this areas interior. The dining table was over by the bay windows and a single door facing the south of the building. The bay windows had small shelf units attached at the bottom of the windows for holding potted plants. Curtains and blinds added to the décor. The flooring in this area was made of multi-patterned and colourful 1-foot square tiles.

The kitchen was more in the pointed area of the pie-shaped room. It contained an island sink for washing dishes and acted as a miniature room divider. Against one wall of the kitchen with ventilation was a self-cleaning, wall mounted oven unit. Beside the oven was a separate stovetop unit. Plenty of cupboard space surrounded the two appliances. Beside these was a huge dual metal door refrigeration unit with the capacity to make ice in an ice-making machine built in one door. The freezer compartment was a fair size for this style of refrigeration unit.

The hallway connecting the three bedrooms, washer and dryer room (*plus closet space*) and main washroom were connected to a small archway opposite the patio doors in the living room. The order was two bedrooms twelve feet by twelve feet, with the main hallway washroom beside these rooms. Again, the same rug material ran through all the bedrooms and the hallway. Only the bathrooms, washer, and dryer room had wooden or tiled floors.

Opposite one of the small bedrooms and connected to the fireplace wall was the master bedroom. Here was a room twenty feet by twenty feet. It had its own washroom and walk-in closet space.

To complete the hallway on the west side of the building was a door leading to the washer and dryer room and additional closet space.

In case of emergency, a door led out the north side of the house from the washer/dryer room. Another door with a short balcony, built off the east side of the hallway, beside the kitchen, to let people out in case of an emergency.

As for the old fences and corrals, he had new ones built to replace these old ones.

The drafting blueprints included a new barn with stables. It also had drawings for a new building constructed opposite the barn and across the lane. These commodes were for any future servants, guests and ranch hands.

The last two items Noah had added were two smaller structures containing power generators. One of these generators housed in an enclosed lean-to, on the west side of the ranch house, provided power for the ranch house during a power outage. The other generator was on the west side of the servant's quarters. It produces electricity for the rest of the buildings on the ranch.

When the project, seven months later, was completed, the whole thing cost around $859,000 in the early 1980's. Noah was truly satisfied with his biggest investment.

The people in the small community of Custard had a chance to come and see the grand opening of the **Nowhere Ranch**. Noah's family and old stage troupe had the privilege of coming and meeting people of the community. GM arranged a family barbeque, horseback riding, dancing and music by a local band.

A local reporter of the **Idaho Sun** had a chance to interview Noah and got GM's picture in the local newspaper. This gave everyone the privilege of meeting Time Magazine and Business Newsweek's youngest entrepreneur.

Noah enjoyed entertaining everyone by treating him or her to a huge bonfire made from the old building materials (*including the old outhouse*). Noah piled dried old wood on top of a buried, flat boulder, a ½-mile away from the new buildings and then set them ablaze. The public enjoyed using it as a wiener and marshmallow roast. To add to the festivities, Noah arranged a small firework displace to go off as soon as the sun set in the west.

After being gone from Red Cliff, California for four months, Noah sent several letters and postcards to his former stage troupe and family members. He encouraged the troupe to come and live in the area of Custard. No one in Red Cliff knew what had happened to him until his letters showed up. Just one day GM had disappeared as if from the surface of the earth. Then when the letters arrived, they were happy to hear he was still alive and they finally found out where he moved too.

This left open the opportunity for Jay and the gang to start several live stage productions or musicals in a new area. Custard's old *Cypress Theatre* sat silent for five years. Its size was thirty feet larger than the Red Bluff Theatre and the acoustic capabilities were unbelievable. If a player on stage whispered, the audience heard their voice as if that player was right beside them. However, if a player screamed aloud, the building had a way of toning down the actor's voice to tolerable hearing levels. This theatre had real potential, despite the subtle drawbacks. The only question was, would his friends be willing to move to a new town or not?

= = =

For the last year and a half after Noah skipped town, Sylvia Winch kept hunting for him. Every time she asked his family members where he was, they kept saying they didn't know. Frustrated but determined to get his money, Sylvia kept up her investigation.

Then one evening in the month of May 1980, she bumped into Shane Hunter, a former high school sex machine whom she hadn't seen in over a year. Striking up a long conversation, they both headed over to one of the local pubs and had a few drinks. In time, one thing led to another and then they were in bed together just like the good old days. Most times Sylvia insisted her male partners wear condoms. On this particular evening, Shane and Sylvia were so drunk that neither of them noticed that Shane didn't put one on. They continually rolled around in the hay until the sun began peeking its crown above the eastern skyline.

Quitting their sexual escapades for the moment both of them showered, dressed and went out for breakfast together. The evenings drinking binge didn't remove the throbbing sensations in their craniums nor the bloodshot eyes they had that morning. Therefore, Sylvia didn't tell Shane what she wanted him for, until she found Noah's hideout.

The answer to where Noah was hiding came to her by chance. Sylvia stopped by the local theatre a couple of months later to see a part of The Red Bluff Players latest performance. While waiting to talk to Jay, she happened to spot some mail on the goodies table. Looking around to see if anyone was watching her, no one did, she flipped through the mail to find a letter from Idaho. The address in the left hand corner was from Custard County and the initials above that address was none other than Noah's initials.

"Aha! Gotcha! Thought you could disappear on me, eh smart guy? I think not!" She copied down the address and slipped out of the theatre unnoticed.

Sylvia tried to contact Shane on his phone – no answer! Therefore, she left a message on the old answering machine for him to meet her at the address in Idaho.

Packing her bags was not easy; she was feeling sick again that morning and she began throwing up. Thinking it was an unrelenting flu bug she had picked up, she held off her plans to travel right away.

The symptoms had continued for almost six weeks. She finally decided to go to the doctor and find an answer to this perplexing problem. What answer she got from the doctor shocked her.

"Well Miss Winch," addressed Doctor Ivan Hapsburg, "you are not sick with any flu bug, virus or even with any food poisoning that we can see."

Sylvia breathed a sigh of relief to this news, but the doctor continued, "You my dear, are pregnant! You've been having morning sickness."

The news struck her like a thunderbolt.

"That's impossible! There was no way I could be pregnant. You're wrong! Do your tests again, a mistake has been made!"

"My dear, we did the tests several times and came up with the same answer. You are with a child - period."

Silence filled the room until, "How far along do you think doc?" Sylvia asked sheepishly.

"Roughly seven to nine weeks," he declared coldly.

Sylvia leaned back into the chair she was sitting in and tried to figure out how this happened to her. The answer seemed to be a fog and was not forth coming!

After thanking the doctor for his help, she left his office.

*Pregnant, of all the stupid things to become, I'm pregnant!* Thinking for a moment a new agenda popped into her head, *Yes, I can use this to my advantage.* Smiling at her new-masterminded strategy, she headed home to pack for the long journey to Custard County, Idaho. However, she was going to leave only when the morning sickness subsided.

# CHAPTER 7

# ALL MINE!

Noah became a bit of a celebrity to the people of Custard, Idaho. He enjoyed the town folk's friendliness and welcoming attitude. The only thing that never escaped his awareness was the undercurrents of family competitiveness to have one's daughter marry the wealthy newcomer. During this time, several single females swooned over GM's brilliant mind and youthful physique. A few parents in the town tried to match make Noah with their daughter. The result was a no go! Despite how strong the tension in the air could be, Noah politely held off all proposals offered.

The Game Master never fell for anyone's tricks. He knew that most of the citizens of Custard were after his pocket book and not really interested in him as an individual.

There were times when fights would break out between competing females wanting his eyes focused on them. Some of these girls would go to extreme lengths to gain GM's attention, like throwing themselves at Noah and almost knocking him off his feet.

One August morning such an event took place. It was on one of these occasions that ten girls attacked this young eighteen-year-old hunk, from all sides of the boardwalk. They all fought '*to get their man*' by piling one on top of another. That's when Noah heard a familiar commanding female voice booming above the frenzied pile up.

The voice ordered all the girls to get off the young man and act their age by '*ceasing and desisting*' their childish pranks. Slowly and quietly, the girls got off Noah. One by one, each girl stood up to see who the new competitor was and what right had this person to interfere with local affairs.

Posed like an admiral with her arms on her hips, Sylvia Winch stood with her legs planted apart projecting her powerful feline presence. At the same moment, she gave off a stare that indicated, '*get your filthy hands off of **my** prize.*' Not knowing what to do, the girls backed off and disappeared like a fast moving mist.

Standing up on shaky legs, Noah picked up his special book. He then proceeded to fix his dishevelled clothes and mussed up hair. He replied, "I guess I should thank you for saving my skin - Miss?" Turing to the woman who helped him, "Well I'll be …" he couldn't believe his eyes, "it's Sylvia Winch! How the heck are you?"

Laughing at his astonishment she said coyly, "Anything for a fellow school mate!" Then breaking into a smile, she continued, "Yes it's me and I'm fine!" She slid her arm through his and both started walking south down the sidewalk together. Some of the local girls saw this action from a distance and fumed with rage, wanting to get even with this old upstart. How dare she interfere with their plans?

"By the way," GM stopped and turned to Sylvia, "What are you doing in this neck of the woods?"

"Well …" thinking out a slick lie quickly, "I bumped into Jay about three weeks ago. During our conversation, your name came up. When I asked why you left town so quickly, Jay avoided answering my question directly. Without giving any details," they continued walking down the street, "all he said was you needed a new place to live. I somewhat repeatedly bugged him to give me all the information about what happened to you to make you leave so fast. Jay avoided my persistent interrogation and tried changing subjects. So I asked him at least where you moved too, he hinted that you were here."

If Noah sensed her skilled lie, he never let on! "I assume you must be hungry from your long trip?"

"Oh yes I am!" she stated most emphatically, "Where is a good burger joint around here? I'm so famished I could eat an entire horse right now!"

"How about we go to **_Richard's Gut Busters_**? You'll be so stuffed by the time you finish the meal!"

"Sounds fantastic, but how far is it from here?" questioned Sylvia.

"It's just a block away. Come on!"

As they both walked and talked en route to the burger parlour, Sylvia lowered her left arm and made a tapping effect, with a flat, open palm, on her left hip. As part of her new scheme, this cue was for Shane, who was hiding in a store watching the two of them pass by, to follow behind them. Noah was unaware of her gesture, but he was wary of her motives. What irked his mind most was why she was here!

"Well I must say I haven't eaten like that for a long time," stated Sylvia. Then letting out a belch of air, she blushed and excused herself. Noah laughed and they both continued talking about what happened in the past few months, when another familiar voice joined them, "Well I'll be! I don't believe it, Noah Body and Sylvia Winch! How are you two?"

Noah and Sylvia stopped talking and looked in the direction of the familiar voice. Standing before them was Shane Hunter.

A little stunned but sensing something cagey may be under foot, Noah never let on about his suspicions of these two gold diggers. Noah stood up and spoke as if in a dumbstruck state of mind, "Shane Hunter, what are you doing here in Custard County?"

After shaking hands, Shane sat down and began to spin a wild tale for the benefit of his two former schoolmates. Although it was well rehearsed, Noah could tell these two were cooking up something not good and that a showdown was about to begin. *I'll be ready for the two of you and what you can dish out*, thought GM confidently. *Let the tournaments begin, I'm game for a new challenge!*

During the reminiscing, Noah interrupted thirty minutes later and offered to get milk shakes all around. The others accepted his offer and stated what flavours they wanted. Just as he was about to go and get their orders, he flicked a small switch at the bottom of his book and left it on the table, observed unknowingly by the others.

"How did I do?" asked Shane in a low voice.

"Better then we rehearsed it," stated Sylvia.

"I hope he doesn't catch on as to why we're here. He …"

"As long as you don't hit the bottle during your stay here, we'll get this guy. I want his money and that's all there is to it. I'll do anything to get it! That's why I intend to go as far as marriage to this wealthy idiot, just to get his money. All ten million dollars of his will be mine! When I have full control over him, I'll have full control over his property and wealth. Then at a later date, I'll divorce him and get everything I can from him, so that I don't have to work ever again."

"As if you ever worked in your life," Shane replied sarcastically with a smirk.

Sylvia fumed and was ready to hit Shane, when Noah came back.

"Now let's see – Sylvia you wanted a chocolate shake!"

"Yes. Thank you dear!"

"Shane yours was also a chocolate – correct?"

"Yep – that's correct. Thank you Noah!"

"You're both welcome. As for me I'm having a vanilla shake." Sitting down again, Noah shut off the switch at the bottom of the book. No one notice him doing it because Noah had practiced this manoeuvre for quite a while. He continued, "This is just like having a shake at the old Franklin Mall." All laughed lightly and enjoyed their thick shakes in silence.

= = =

For his own protection, Noah had to purchase a tape recorder that was small enough to be concealed in an old book and yet powerful enough to pick up voices within a ten-foot radius. In the book he was carrying was such a concealed device. He began to have some of the parents in the town, pull off all kinds of stunts to get this wealthy lad to marry their daughters. Some of the schemes or manipulations they used were just unbelievable. By using the tape recorder, he was able to deflect any false claims some of the town folks used against him. They would make accusations about Noah and claimed he made this agreement or that agreement, while it was not so! By using the concealed tape recorder, and recording people's conversations with him, he could expose their lies and avoid lawsuits.

Since GM was suspicious of these two former school chums, he used the recorder to get their every conversation after he left the table. *This will be good ammunition for later on*, he thought to himself. Little did Noah realize how important these tapes would become!

After leaving Richard's place, the three walked around Custard and talked about all kinds of subjects. As time passed on, rumbling tummies indicated time for dinner. Thinking of the finest restaurant in town, Noah asked if the two money grabbers would join him. They were delighted to. So they headed to **Sing Soot's Oriental Cuisine**.

This was a darker place than the burger joint and had an oriental classiness to it. Sing Soot was the owner and he always enjoyed Noah's visits to his restaurant. His two daughters and one son were already happily married. Mr. Soot enjoyed his last few remaining years serving excellent Chinese cuisine to the locals. The only problem he had was the financing for the updating of the building. Unknown to the entire community, Noah loved Mr. Soot's food so much; he gave Mr. Soot the funds to refurbish the restaurant. There was one simple request from Noah – Sing didn't have to pay back GM the money. Because of GM's generous nature, Mr. Soot always made sure that Noah had a special table reserved for him whenever he came to eat. Noah tried to make it a habit to eat there at least once every seven to ten days.

When Mr. Soot saw Noah coming with some friends, his excitement mounted. He ran to GM and gave him a friendly handshake with that broad smile of his. Sing personally waited on Noah every time he showed up. Seeing he was with company, Noah introduced his former school chums to Mr. Soot. Excited that GM was there, Mr. Soot told Noah about a new curry dish he wanted to try out. Noah said he was delighted to try this new cuisine. Then Mr. Soot happily encouraged GM to come to his special table reserved for him.

All the oriental designed rice paper lamps, were either electrical or candle style, added soft lighting everywhere. A large fish aquarium provided a wall divider between the entrance of the building and the seating area. Tropical fish swam around happily observing the customers or chasing each other around.

On the walls and hanging off the ceiling were hand painted silk tapestries. They depicted various scenes of China, animals or fish. The lighting in the building back lit some of these tapestries and added beauty to the place.

Soft easy listening or oriental music played in the background. As this music played, the sound didn't seem to come from any one location; it rebounded and felt like the melody flowed throughout the entire building; just as a river flows; and one couldn't locate the exact location of the orchestra pit.

Yes, Mr. Soot's restaurant made customers feel welcome as well as relaxed while they dined. Most times Mr. Soot's restaurant was so full with customers, many people lined up outside to enjoy his special cuisines. Today, only a handful of people were here.

The table that Mister Soot seated Noah was near the kitchen doors and close to the bar.

"I'm impressed with your place Mr. Soot," stated Sylvia as she continued to look around. "You've decorated this establishment with such beautiful and delicate artwork. I'm very impressed!"

Speaking perfect and clear English, Mister Soot replied while bowing, "Thank you Miss. Thank you!" He handed out the menus, "Would anyone want anything to drink from the bar?"

Shane requested a beer; Noah chose a glass of red wine and Sylvia decided to stick with water. As Mr. Soot left to fill everyone's request, the trio began looking through the menu and deciding on various meals. When Sing returned, everyone made his or her choice of meal and informed Sing what it was. Noah definitely wanted to try Sing's new chicken vegetable noodle curry dish.

When Mr. Soot left to cook and fill the orders, the trio's conversations continued. Still carrying his book, GM set it down so that the two schemer's voices recorded clearly. Without the knowledge of the others, GM flipped the '*on*' switch on this hidden recorder and stated that he had to excuse himself to use the restroom for a moment.

This was when the two scoundrels began to go over the plot of how they would convince Noah to marry Sylvia so she had access to his money. Then when the time was right, she would divorce him and take all his wealth and property from him.

Shane stated that he wanted to marry Sylvia after the divorcing took place. All Sylvia wanted from Shane was the wild kinky sex they had and nothing more. Then the two of them made a pact. If time had gone by and neither of them caught in their sexual acts; then both of them would continue to sneak around and cheat on Noah. Nevertheless, because she was pregnant at this period, she never spoke up about the pregnancy nor did she say it aloud. Their conversation ended when Noah returned eleven minutes later.

Flicking the '*off*' switch on the recorder with the subtle movement of a finger, Noah slipped his book into his large coat pocket. Again, the others never noticed his sleight of hand techniques.

Their meals arrived to their table a minute later, to hearty appetites.

*What an interesting evening this will become*; thought GM.

When Sylvia left the restaurant to get some sleep in her motel room, Noah invited Shane to stay for several more drinks. After a while, Shane became drunk and needed to excuse himself to use the washroom. Noah then rewound the tape and listened to it. What he had heard didn't startle him in the least, but it gave him an idea. Writing up a simple contract on a small piece of blank paper, GM wanted to get Shane to sign the document.

Staggering as he returned, Shane wanted another drink before going to bed. GM presented Shane with the contract for him to sign. Shane didn't know what he had agreed too or even signed that evening. Noah then kept the paper and hoped to use it in the future.

Noah and Mister Soot then proceeded to assist Shane to a local taxicab and instructed the driver to deliver the boy to his motel.

Noah paid and thanked Mr. Soot for the great evening. He then headed back to his ranch. Once home he rewound the tape again and listened to the entire conspirator's conversations. *I knew they were up to something rotten. What a cabal they've formed*, thought Noah to himself. Not one to avoid a challenge, unless it meant harming or killing someone, GM began making counter plans of his own to rid him of these plotters.

In a flash, he came up with a brilliant idea. He would design a simple quiz game to test the minds of all single women who wanted to marry him. The questions would not be easy to solve. In three days' time, this game would take place!

= = =

Going to the local paper early in the morning, Noah placed an ad for all single local girls, between the ages of 17 and 22, who wanted to marry him, had to be able to answer four problems correctly or at least have 75% of them correct. The contest would start the next Thursday at noon. Noah would ascertain a winner by the answers they gave. The winning female had to be ready to married him that Saturday afternoon. To give competitors a chance to answer the quiz, Noah had the paper print the problems ahead of time, while excluding the sources.

The questions that were printed were as follows:

1) *When and what was the worst plague to strike in the twentieth century and how many people did it exterminate?*

2) *What 1929 invention did Americans invent which is used and enjoyed by everyone today?*

3) *A mountain I have never climbed, but forced, I had to descend one. Who am I?*

4) *I once saw the sun, but never twice in lore. I was soft, then hard, then soft once more. What event describes me and evens a score?*[5]

The contest GM knew would narrow any successor down to Sylvia only. She was a mastermind at finding answers and scheming what she wanted, she'd do anything to get the feedback needed to win. To make it truly challenging, Noah

---

[5]   Can you an answer to the last riddle? Go to Appendix "E" to solve this brainteaser.

created the last two riddles requiring exegesis to understand and solve them properly.

Next thing Noah had to do was to find an attorney to assist him in writing up a cleverly worded, special duplicate document. To make this document legal would require the signatures of him, Sylvia and two witnesses. This prevented her in the future from using any legal means in order to confiscate all his funds, which he obtained over the years. The document would stick out from beneath the signing book, at the wedding service, so that those signing it would not see what settlements the document stated.

"Let the combat begin!" exclaimed GM.

The day arrived in its entire splendour. Thirty-five females arrived to compete. Highly excited female voices crowded into the high school gymnasium and waited to compare their answers to those in the quiz. Some of the women tried to predict who the winner might be, or at least narrow it down to a few possible candidates. Even Sylvia was in amongst them, hoping and determined to be the winner.

When Noah entered the centre of the room and he sat down on a podium chair. He waited patiently. A hush descended over the crowded room and all hopeful eyes focused on the prize. After a moment of silence, Noah stood up and began to lay down a few simple regulations.

"Ladies, I must welcome you all to an exciting and unusual contest. The beautiful faces and fantastic figures I see before me already make it challenging me to continue this event. I know how you all feel and the high energy in this auditorium proves that point."

Some giggles and light laughs came from the contestants.

Turning serious, "Unfortunately, like all sporting events or games, there will be losers and only one winner. One of you lovely creatures will have the privilege of being a winner and my future bride. As for the rest of you, I must apologize to you now and hope nothing more than the best for you all. If everyone is ready, here are a few rules!"

"OK. The first rule: Any female that has the correct answer to the questions provided in the paper can stay in the gymnasium for the next question. The second rule: If anyone has a wrong answer or is missing information in their answers, they have lost the contest and must leave the room immediately before the next question begins. This would narrow down who would be the final combatants and eventually to the one possible winner. To make the rules simple, everyone must agree to the rules - no exceptions! Do you **all** agree?"

Many heads nodded in agreement and a few said 'yes' at the same time.

"If anyone here doesn't agree with these simple rules, you may leave the gym now and no one will think the worst of you."

No one left.

"Then, let the competition begin!" GM returned to his chair.

"The first question asked was: *When and what was the worst plague to strike in the twentieth century and how many people did it exterminate?*" He paused before revealing the answer. All eyes and ears were upon him.

Knowing everyone would get the first one right, he gave the following: "The answer to this question requires a three part answer. You must have those three parts correct before going forward. If one part of your answer is wrong or missing one correct part of the answer, then you must leave the room. The answer: In 1918, the Spanish Influenza swept across many countries. It exterminated approximately 20 million people worldwide." Pausing again he then continued, "If your answer has the three items mentioned; **1918**, the **Spanish Influenza** and **approximately 20 million deaths**; you may stay. If your answer was incorrect in any way or you missed any part of the answer just mentioned, you must leave now!"

Five girls left the room with their heads looking down and their faces forlorn, the rest snickered at the losers as they left and then waited for the contest to continue.

When these women had left the gymnasium, then GM repeated the second question. "The second question: *What 1929 invention did Americans invent which is used and enjoyed by everyone today?*" He paused again before revealing the answer. All remaining eyes were upon him. This time he knew more would get this question wrong.

Therefore, he revealed the answer as follows, "The American invention was the car radio. In was made in 1929 and is still installed in automobiles today." Pausing again he then continued, "If your answer was the same as I've given - **the car radio**; you may stay. If your answer was incorrect, you must leave now!"

Many groans and mumbled swear words flooded the room. When the majority of the women filed out of the buildings doors, some fights and nasty words exchanged outside the building by the losers. This now left only five women remaining - Sylvia being one of them.

Noah was now happy that the second question eliminated the majority of the contestants, so he changed the rules for the last two questions.

"To make the next question a bit of a hurdle, I'm going to repeat the question. Instead of me giving the correct answer immediately, I'll give you lovely lassies a chance to share your answers aloud. The original rules still apply. Does this sound reasonable to everyone? Please form a straight line."

The five women agreed with the terms and made a line up before him.

Repeating the third question Noah said, "The third question: *A mountain I've never climbed but forced, I had to descend one. Who am I?*"

*I can't wait to give my answer first*, thought Sylvia. Nevertheless, she was flabbergasted to see that Noah chose the youngest female to give her answer first.

Noah did this because he knew it would irk Sylvia's nerves to go last.

Sylvia was starting to heat up at the fact an insolent seventeen year old had gone before her high and mightiness. *How dare that moron not make me go first! Maturity before youth I always say!*

The first female thought it was an American explore in the Antarctic. After a quick explanation to her answer, she then waited for Noah to say something. Saying nothing, all Noah did was turn his attention to the second contestant and said, "Your answer is…?"

Sylvia's blood pressure increased a notch or two. Slowly steam percolated from under her collar. *What are you doing? I was supposed to go next. Ugh – You're pissing me off buster!*

The second woman thought the teenager was wrong and stated that fact. She then figured the correct answer referred to Gandhi. Saying nothing, Noah turned his attention to the third contestant and said, "And your answer is…?"

Sylvia's blood began boiling and steam jetted out of her ears!

The next two women figured they had the correct answers and stated their cases. Again after each woman's explanation, Noah didn't respond except to finally turn his attention to Sylvia and said, "And your answer would be…?"

By now Sylvia, who was extremely frustrated, exactly as Noah had predicted would happen. To Sylvia these four insolent youngsters went before her, how dare they do that. Narrowing her eyes, her volcanic fury made her top pop. The only word she squeezed through her clenched teeth was "**NOAH…!**" Nothing else came from her mouth (*except some steam*).

Feeling the temperature rising in the room, GM smiled and congratulated Sylvia for being the winner. The correct answer was the **Biblical Noah**. He dismissed the other girls who scowled at Sylvia for winning and stormed off to inform the others of the fixed quiz.

As for Sylvia, she just stood there stupefied and no longer enraged. She couldn't believe she had won let alone played this stupid game with Noah. The idea of winning hadn't sunk into her brain yet and the fact that she was going to marry him that Saturday – two days away.

"Well I guess we should work on the wedding arrangements. Shouldn't we?" declared Noah.

"Uh … Yes I guess we should," answered Sylvia still dazed.

They were both married in a local United Church on August 16th, 1980.

During the signing of the church register and marriage license, Noah had his special documents set up for her signature as well. No one paid much attention to the special documents Noah had created with his attorney.

Prearranged ahead of time, was the photo shoot. In order to get better pictures of the bridal party, the signing table needed removal. Noah's best man was Jay, who assisted in moving the signing table, while slipping the special documents into his suit pocket. Jay would give these documents to Noah later on while no one noticed.

Everyone invited to an evening of dinner and dancing at the local dance hall. Noah's family was there also. From Sylvia's family came her only living relatives, her aunt and uncle along with her father in a wheelchair. Although Connie Body objected to her youngest son's choice of wife, she didn't interfere. Noah reassured his mother that he had everything taken care of and she shouldn't worry, he could take care of himself.

Except for those few females who lost the contest and protested in silence by not attending the wedding ceremony, most of the town attended the evening meal and dance with the newly married couple. Many wedding presents were stacked on a table. This encouraged the new lovebirds to enjoy their new life together.

They both put on a show for everyone in attendance when hugging, kissing, picture taking and dancing. Like a phoney mirage, this so-called love nest put on the best illusion of joyful bliss, while underneath frothed a cauldron of poisonous venom and burning brimstone.

After all said and done, Noah picked Sylvia up according to human tradition and walked her over the threshold into the new ranch house. Although Sylvia had to put up with the kissing and dancing with her new mate, all she really wanted was Noah's ten million dollars. As far as she was concerned, it was all hers and none of it belonged to her new husband. When she was taking across the threshold, she decided instantaneously she was laying down the ground rules as soon as Noah set her down.

First, she was not going to sleep with Noah in any way, shape, or form.

Second, all she wanted was for him to be out of her face so she could do whatever she wanted.

Third, he had to give her everything she demanded, when she demanded it.

Noah heard her demands, but ignored them. When she finished, being her new husband and partner, he too laid down certain ground rules.

First, he built, owned the deed to and paid for the homestead, she couldn't demand anything; since she was not there at the time and he built the place.

Second, she will only utilize what he gives her and never employ childish tactics to get what she wants.

Third, he was happy never to sleep with her at all or for any reason.

Fourth, he was only going to give her an allowance of financing as he deemed fit to give her at a specified time and not when she squawked for it.

After that, the war of wits between these Body family members would continue from their wedding night for some 18 or so years. To prevent other people seeing this war zone, both combatants had to put on a façade of a loving and caring family. This was to conceal the real facts of what their counterfeit marriage was truly like.

Through it all, Sylvia believed everything was *all hers* and none of it belonged to Noah.

# CHAPTER 8

# A New Body Cometh

When it came to their honeymoon, Sylvia put on a stunning Academy Award performance for all to see. The cruise ship this couple traveled on took them through various ports of call within the Caribbean area. It was while they were on this cruise that each antagonist gave a pet name to the other out of earshot from other passengers. Sylvia loved to call him a '*Moron*' or '*Retard*', while Noah called her a '*Nutcase*' or '*Swamp Cabbage*'.

After their two weeks of fun, both exhausted cruisers couldn't wait to go back to the ranch. During all this time, Noah never let on that he already knew the mastermind's schemes. Without revealing anything, Noah also had a plan of his own which he was willing to implement before their first anniversary came to its conclusion. He felt he was ready to take action!

The next morning the sun was rising through a clear glass sky. Various shades of colour smoothly blended and transformed into slow motion swirls, which finally conclude to the hue of blue. While watching the rising sun, Noah enjoyed his breakfast of eggs, toast and homemade hash browns. By the time the sky turned its familiar blue, Noah sat at the kitchen island reading the stock market reports in the newspaper and sipping a hot cup of coffee.

Sylvia had just awakened and slowly lumbered into the kitchen, yawning, stretching and looking forward to a scrumptious meal. As she walked past, Noah noticed that her stomach was sticking out a little bigger than since the wedding of fifteen days ago. He just couldn't wait to get a dig into her.

"I see that being married is really agreeable for you – '*Nutcase*'," stated Noah with a sarcastic smirk.

"What do you mean - *Retard*?" snarled back Sylvia.

"You're gaining beach ball frontage, dear. Eating too much of that cruise cuisine can cause those results you have!" Noah enjoyed rubbing in his comment, then he added more sarcasm to it. "I've heard of people gaining weight after they are married, but I do swear, a person would think you were in a major race to join the fat, smelly Sea Lions off the west coast. Keep it up and we'll have to ship you to Alaska," he snickered to himself. Since Sylvia wanted nothing to do with him since the wedding, he was going to enjoy getting his digs into this selfish and greedy lowlife.

Sylvia grabbed a bowl of cereal with milk, half a grapefruit and headed over to the kitchen table to eat them.

"Oh, Hardy-har-har! I applaud your so-called originality," she gestured with a gag reflex. "How long did it take you to come up with that one? Maybe you should go to Alaska instead of me. You're also gaining a few love handles of your own, blubber boy!" She was waiting for the right moment to spring her trap.

"No, I could come up with something else but that would continue to drive you normal. I just happened to notice that your tummy is getting bigger, that's all. Besides, who wants to spoil a wonderful day? You missed watching a fantastic sunrise! Maybe you should just ease off those extra snacks you enjoy consuming at all hours of the night. That way you can keep your splendid hourglass figure all the time *Swamp Cabbage.*"

Plunking her butt down on a kitchen chair to be further away from Noah, she knew this was the time to attack aggressively, "For your information Mister Know-it-All, it is not because of snack food that I'm gaining weight *Skunk Breath.* It is because - I'm pregnant - you *Simpleton!*"

Noah almost choked on a mouthful of hot coffee, "**What!**" Coughing to clear his airways that just had fluid flow into them, Noah managed to squeak out, "You're pregnant?" The thunderbolt from this news hit him like a sledgehammer.

Sylvia relished in the thought of shocking her new hubby. She wasn't finished yet insulting this fool of a bright humanoid. Without saying a word, she continued consuming her breakfast, grinning to herself.

"There's no way you could be pregnant. I didn't impregnate you! In fact, neither of us sleeps together at night, we both have separate bedrooms. There's no way you could be pregnant!"

"Oh but I am - you *Lamebrain!* And yes it can be done," seethed Sylvia with glee and rubbing salt in a wound. She just dropped a bombshell on Noah's head and she knew the revelation had jolted him. She continued to drill her point deeper into the wound, "To have a child is not hard. Any male can get a female pregnant. It just boils down to the question as to who's the father of the child." She now beamed with the joy of destroying GM's so-called beautiful morning.

Noah couldn't believe his ears. His mind raced through various possibilities and came up with only one solution. "So you already knew you were pregnant, before you married me, is that it?"

Enjoying the stunned look and expression on Noah's face, she dug into the grapefruit and said scornfully, "Well done *Sherlock Holmes*! You've finally solved the obvious crime of the decade! Congratulations! You're looking at me like I know who got me in this condition – right?"

"Now that you've mentioned it, yes, I've been wondering …" Noah never completed his sentence.

With great speed, she cut him off with, "At this point in time, I don't know and I don't give a shit! All I do is just informing people it is your child and no one else will know the difference."

"So how far along are you? When is the child due?" Noah demanded to know.

Finishing her grapefruit and her cereal, she addressed his questions. "According to the doctor, he thinks I'm around 15 weeks. In my mind, I think I'm closer to 17. I'll be due sometime in the first two weeks of January. It doesn't matter either way, all I know is that I'll be having a child in a few months and we'll have to raise the baby in a proper family setting, not an Orang-utan Zoo! So get used to the idea of being a father, *Reject*." Then Sylvia put her garbage in the kitchen garbage can, her dishes in the dishwasher and left Noah in the kitchen to stew over this revelation, alone.

By now, Noah's shock had worn off. The fact that he found out she was already pregnant and she hid this very information, infuriated him. All of GM's plans to get Sylvia for her scheming a year after the marriage, were altered by this turn of events. The only reason he could see as to why she married him so fast was for all of his money. Then she wanted the entire property and to take his family name for her child. Although he was angry with this manipulating money grabber, he realized he had to accept this new trial even though the child was not his. Therefore, he prepared himself ahead of time by taking courses and reading books on how to raise a child.

Later that afternoon, Noah went for a solo walk to Seven Mile Hill in order to clear his mind from this new disturbing turn of events. In the meantime, Sylvia took the family car into Custard to meet up with Shane in the local Gut Busters.

Pausing at the fence around the horse corral, Noah began reflecting about his family and the years gone by. Such things came to his mind like the marriage of his oldest brother Calvin in June of 1970. Noah had the privilege of being the ring bearer for that ceremony as a seven year old. Then his sister Shirley got married in July of 1973. Again, he was the ring bearer for her ceremony, at the age of ten. Taze got married in March of 1977, while his father passed away in September of the same year. Now he was married and with a child on the way. The only one left of the family to get married would be his older sister – Rose.

Continuing his slow walk toward the split rocks at Seven Mile Hill, Noah had a new question enter into his mind. *Now what do I do next?*

Staring off into the valley below, his mind began strategizing how to run the ranch properly; "I should hire people to help me run the horse ranch and care for the family!"

Putting together a team of different people and positions was going to be a challenge. Like a chef for most meals and a couple of house cleaners to clean the ranch house and staff accommodations. A gardener to maintain the lawns and gardens, along with several ranch hands for horse training; this list and others not yet mentioned were all the helping hands Noah needed to keep the place running. Although it would cost money, GM was not worried. He knew Sylvia would not be able to handle everything by herself especially in her recent condition. The more hands the merrier! *Yes, I'll start hiring people right away. Since I control the cash flow, that witch will have nothing to say about the matter!* Pivoting on his heels, GM tore back to the ranch house in order to drive down town to enquire for various labourers.

As Noah interviewed various people for the jobs he had in mind, he realized that he would have to use up to seven million dollars over a three-year period. By year five onward, GM calculated he would be receiving the returns for this large equine enterprise. He would use part of the funds to pay his hard working staff (*including benefits and bonuses*).

Sylvia was not her usual self. Being pregnant had changed her outlook on life and upset her hormonal balance. Becoming a mother pissed her off since she had all these plans for stealing

Noah's money. Now that a child was on the way and she was not quite sure whom the father was, she was going to have to hold off seeing Shane for a while. At least until the child has weaned off breast-feeding.

As soon as Sylvia entered the fast food joint, Shane couldn't keep his hands off her.

Finally, Sylvia had to tell the boy to cool down. Too many people in the community knew she was married to Noah and she feared they would report to him about their liaison. She told Shane wait for a full year or two, and then they would restart their covert lustful liaison were it last left off.

Shane was not sure why they had to cut back from each other for two years.

Sylvia had to explain to him that she was expecting Noah's child.

The news hit Shane like a ton of bricks. When he spoke again after five minutes of silence, he didn't like the arrangement. However, relenting to this news, he agreed to wait until the two years had passed.

As much as Sylvia didn't want to hurt her favourite sex partner, she could no longer hide the truth. By confessing this information to Shane, gave her the time needed to raise the little one, until they could meet again.

When they left the fast food joint, they each left separately to not arouse any local spy's suspicions.

Noah called his mother the next day to talk to her. He made sure that Sylvia's elephant ears were not around to hear the conversation.

"…Son is there a problem? I've already told you that I didn't like that woman from the beginning. She's a lazy schemer, a gold digger and I've never trusted her. Besides, how could you forget her reputation out here? Why did you do it – Nobby?"

"Ma – I know how you feel, but I made the choice and I've got to live with it. *Nemesis* thinks all I have is $10 million dollars. She thinks that flaunting the old Time Magazine article about me and waving it around every time gives her all access to any amount of money she wants. She thinks I'll hand it all to her inside a golden chalice."

"Son - how much money has gone to her so far? Hopefully not all of the $10 million?" asked the concerned Connie.

"All I gave her so far was $200,000 to start with. If she spends it all, before the years out, then she'll have to wait until next year for any more moneys. This is how I will control that splurging spree in her genes. As for the rest of the $70 million, it is stashed away safely!"

"Did I hear you correctly - **$70 million?**"

"That's correct Ma! Please don't go telling everyone you know about this information. I believe that the *Scumbag* has spies watching my every move. *'Madame Annoyance'* thinks all I have is the $10 million. In reality, I had increased that amount to well over $70 million before I left from Red Cliff. Remember Ma, I have control over the financing and she will only spend what I want her to spend, not what amount she demands."

"Good for you son, you keep that wretched dog on a tight leash! Don't let her get those sharp claws of hers on your treasure trove! As for me, I will never say a word about how much you have." After a pause, Connie asked, "Was there something else you wanted to share son?"

"The only thing that is new, is the fact she informed me two mornings ago that she is pregnant," replied Noah.

Connie responded to this new turn of events, "**Pregnant - by whom?** Surly the child is not yours?"

"No the child is not mine! I don't know who the child's father is yet. *'Miss Vexation'* has never slept with me since our wedding night. She doesn't care who the real father is anyway! All I know is, she is after all the money I've accumulated through the stock markets and then she astounds me with this new trial. The only reason I could see she wanted to be married so quickly, was to give the child a family name. So she chose me as her prime target."

"Oh son!" exclaimed Connie. "Why did you get involved with this nut case? Didn't you know she would pull this kind of stunt?"

"Ma - don't panic or worry. I didn't know she was pregnant until two days ago. The tsunami effect from such news hit me a low blow. If I had known she was going to pull off this stunt, I'd never have married her. However, I did have plans in place! Since a child is on its way, my plans will not commence until the youngster turns eighteen. So don't panic or worry! I've got this under my control."

"You know how I worry about all you kids. All a mother every wants is for her children to have happy families of their own. Listen *Nobby*, if everything starts falling apart, your welcome to come here with the little one any time you wish. Just leave that scumbag of a tart at the ranch – OK?"

"You bet ma. I'll make sure that '*Wicked Witch*' never visits you. I love you, Ma!" stated Noah.

"I love you too son. May you have all the best, despite being near that crony of ill repute! Bye for now sweetheart!" exclaimed Connie.

"Bye, Ma!" Noah said laughing, before hanging up the phone.

= = =

As the day arrived, Sylvia was in the laundry room when the unexpected hit. She was drying clothes in the dryer. When she rested her hands on the vibrating dryer, the reverberations traveled through her body and gave a slight tingling sensation through her womb. It was 11:26 pm, when suddenly and without warning, her water broke. Not long after she then felt the labour, pains hit with great intensity. Sylvia cried out for Noah to assist her.

Noah walked over to see what the problem was now. When he saw the water on the floor flowing towards the floor drain and Sylvia almost doubled over in pain, he knew the baby was on its way. Helping Sylvia to stand up, he took her to a chair to rest, while he called the hospital and informed them that they were on their way.

He next ran to warm up the truck and clean off the excessive snow build up.

Assisting Sylvia to the truck wasn't easy. Every now and then, she cried out in pain. Measuring the time intervals of

6 minutes between contractions, Noah would have to hustle before the child arrived.

Noah had to drive Sylvia through a snow blizzard that January. Her contractions were now coming every 5 minutes and she was ready to assassinate her hubby because of the pain. To keep herself calm, she continued her breathing exercises between contractions while Noah raced towards Custard.

Flying through the snowstorm in four-wheel drive, Noah made it to the hospital in 18 minutes (*usually it takes 25 minutes to reach town at a regular speed*). Sylvia, with her contractions now down to 2 minutes, she carted down to the delivery room to give birth. The child was coming whether either parent was ready or not.

Before Noah could get a hospital gown on, the baby girl arrived within moments.

As Noah entered the delivery room, the event was all over. He missed the whole procedure and was upset with himself because he wanted to observer the entire process.

Doctor Benson spoke while smiling, "That has to be one of the fastest deliveries I've ever done! Oh, there you are Mister Body! Congratulations to the two of you. You are the proud parents of a healthy baby girl. She weighs in at 9 lbs. She was also born at 3 minutes past midnight January 4th, 1981."

"A baby girl!" said Noah excitedly. Looking towards his wife, who was holding the baby, he said the following, "Well done dear! She's a beauty!" he kissed Nemesis on the forehead.

Smiling she replied, "Yes! She is truly a real doll." In a more loving manner, she continued, "She will be a blessing in disguise and a wonderful flower to nurture!"

Through all the excitement, Nurse Stacey asked, "Mister and Misses Body have you chosen a name for your precious bundle of joy?"

"Yes, we have decided…," stated Sylvia.

She looked into Noah's eyes and said, "We've decided to call her: ***Rutah Allison Body!***"

Noah agreed by nodding his head and silently smiled back.

As the nurse recorded the new name on the birth certificate, the doctor spoke again, "May I congratulate you again, on a beautiful baby girl!"

"Thank you" both parents said at the same time.

Noah and Sylvia had temporally called a truce with each other. It was because a new body had come into the world. This precious little one would need lots of loving and caring.


After a few minutes, Noah had the privilege to hold his newly bundled daughter. He hummed a little tune to his daughter, as he held this fragile package gentle in his strong arms.

As for the baby Rutah, she quietly sucked on her tiny thumb.

Slowly walking around the room, a few hours later, while keeping out of earshot of the exhausted *Nuisance* who was still talking to the doctor, Noah spoke these consoling words under his breath to the new born; "Even though you are not biologically my daughter, I promise you Rutah, I will treat you as if you were my very own. I will love you, care for you and educate you to the best of my abilities. That is my promise to you - my precious hazel eyed *Puddin'*."

The calm voice and humming from Noah had a sleepy effect on the little infant. Even though Rutah didn't understand a single word her father spoke, she yawned, stretched and fell asleep in her father's warm arms.

Noah then kissed his sleeping princess on the forehead before returning the infant to her mother's waiting arms.

This was a special day of joy for both parents.

# CHAPTER 9

# The Little Charmers

Just as if she was a chip off the old Body block, Rutah was an exceptional baby, which any parent would love to have as his or her own child. Similar to Noah when he was an infant, Rutah slept through the entire night without waking up. Because of this, the first few weeks of having this little one home, caused Sylvia concern about the baby.

"I thought babies always woke up at different times of the night?" questioned the worried Sylvia.

"It is true that some infants wake up at different intervals Mrs. Body," confirmed Doctor Benson. "But you have a child that is one of those exceptions to that rule. Look, if you check on your child and she is still breathing while she sleeps, then she is fine. Stop worrying! She's alive and well. Not all parents have the privilege of a child that can do that," he stated bluntly and reassuringly.

Breathing a sigh of relief, Sylvia said, "Ok doctor, you're the boss. Thank you for helping me to calm my fears."

"You're welcome Mrs. Body. If there are any problems with the young one in the future, please don't hesitate to call me, day or night. Ok!"

"Yes doctor! Thank you again!"

In time, Sylvia learned to relax and accept the fact that Rutah liked to awaken in the morning hours with the rest of the family.

Noah enjoyed taking care of his new daughter. He bathed her, fed her, gently massaged her little body and even changed her smelly diapers without complaint. This never bothered him in any way, being a father would have its vicissitudes. So far, GM loved this small person and he slowly introduced Rutah to playing games.

One of the things parents like to do is to get their young ones to laugh or just smile. In time, Noah found many ways to have Rutah laughing, giggling or smiling. A real bond began to form between father and daughter.

As for Sylvia, she waited patiently for the year to finish. She wanted desperately to sleep with Shane; she slowly gave up on taking care of Rutah. Although it did take time, one thing *Nemesis* did was to drop the breast-feeding of Rutah, which lasted until 18 months passed.

At the designated time, Sylvia slipped out of the ranch to seek out a familiar face. Noah spotted her leaving the farm and suspected her motive. He called his new detective friend to follow her and record her every movement.

*Was my sex maniac in the area or not?* Driving to the Gut Busters, Sylvia couldn't wait to see Shane again, a year after their agreement. When she entered the establishment, she didn't see him right away.

Thinking he may have forgotten her, Sylvia was ready to leave after twenty minutes, as a familiar voice spoke to her from behind. It was Shane! Turning around, looking into his blue-green eyes and smiling, she saw the old spark flash forth for the briefest of moments. Shane smiled back. He saw the same glint in her dark brown eyes, a flare of energetic life that both of them needed and looked forward to these past weeks. They quietly left the fast food joint and headed to a motel for a night of fun. The prey never suspected of that a pair of paid invisible dark eyes tailed and videotaped them.

It was the next morning that Shane informed Sylvia that he had to go away for a year or so. He promised to drop by as soon as his new job gave him vacation time to travel!

For a rotund man, detective Harry Sampson was the best in his field. This dark brown-eyed detective knew how to hide or camouflage his movements and disguise his appearance. Noah hired him not long after the Sing's restaurant escapade with Shane. Since Sylvia wanted to hold back on having Shane as a bed partner until her child was born. GM had Harry follow Shane and record his every sexual encounter. What Harry collected over the past year was giving Noah the ammunition he needed at a future time. All of the video and cassette tapes evidence was in a secret safe, hidden inside the staff quarter's office. Noah made sure he paid Harry well. As for Harry, he would do any work for Noah at anytime, anywhere. Noah needed another 17 or so years to complete his formulated plan and knock out two useless opponents at the same time.

Harry Sampson went as far as to follow Shane around and video tape him with various sex collaborates in **Los Angeles**, **California**. This stock footage Noah also placed inside the same safe along with Sylvia's videos.

= = =

By the time Rutah was two years of age, Sylvia didn't want to be raising a troublesome child in her mind. She pushed the toddler away and wanted nothing to do with her. To make matters worse, she would yell or scream insults at the tyke. These psychological attacks took their toll on the toddler especially her mother's put-downs as an inferior and useless dog. Her vicious attacks happened every time she saw Rutah. Sylvia enjoyed tormenting the girl no matter if the child was having fun, sleeping or just playing with her toys. As time passed, Sylvia went as far as to attack or kill some of Rutah's favourite pets. Somehow, in her warped mind, Sylvia felt this would get the point across that she hated the brat.

Although not old enough at this age to understand her mother's irrational emotions and the severe rejection of her personage, Rutah turned to the only person she could for help and guidance her father. Several times, she was crying her little eyes out while seeking her father. She thought she had done something bad, but not understanding what it was.

Bumping into one of the maids, this young woman felt sorry for the tyke. Therefore, she took Rutah in her arms and carried her to her father. When the house cleaner found Rutah's father in the garden, she told her employer what she overheard

Sylvia doing to the child. Rutah's tears caused Noah's heart to sink in sympathy. It also indicated that another vicious attack had come from *Nemesis*. Thanking the maid for her help and letting her go back to her work, Noah was ready to confront his villainous wife in order to straighten her out about child rearing. However, GM first held onto his precious one and comforted his daughter the best way he could.

"There, there, *Sweetheart*. Papa loves you! Don't let that big bad wolf of a mother scare you anymore. To me you are my radiant princess. You're a smart and beautiful flower, blossoming into a young woman. One day you will be able prove that you're not what mama claims."

Rutah kept sniffling and wiping away her tears. The more Noah reassured her she was the opposite of what her mother stated the more Rutah clung to her papa for love and comfort.

"Would you like to help out papa with a small project?" questioned GM, in order for the child to get her mind off her mother's attacks.

Rutah smiled and shook her head 'yes'.

"Ok then, just come with me!" smiled Noah, as he kissed Rutah to reassure her of his love.

Going out to a garden were the fresh earth had being turned over, Noah got Rutah to help him transplant some flowers he purchased earlier. He explained how and where to put each flower. Rutah found it fun and educational at the same time. When she got tired, Noah let her sleep in a shady spot while he finished the planting.

As Rutah slept, Noah went to address Sylvia about her attitude towards their daughter when the phone rang. It was

Rose, his sister. She told Noah she was getting married in two weeks and she wanted Noah to come. Noah agreed and asked if Rutah could come along. Rose said definitely yes!

After the phone call, Noah arranged for Harry to watch over sly Sylvia while he and Rutah would go to his youngest sister's wedding. Next, Noah got airline tickets for the two of them to go to **Kawaihae Bay**, **Hawaii**. Noah never bothered to tell *Swamp Cabbage* about the wedding. Besides, Sylvia would not even care to go, not with all the new sex partners she had accumulated lately!

At the wedding little Rutah looked like a beautiful angel with flowers braided in her hair, clean yellow Hawaiian printed dress and sandals.

When any photographs taken, Rutah enjoyed posing in several camera shots and she seemed to beam before the lens. Being a well-behaved child, she sometimes was in the picture with her father, her aunt Rose or sometimes just by herself. In one scene, she had blown a kiss to the camera and everyone there caught it. Rutah became the envy of most of the other parents. They wished their children behaved themselves and look so clean all the time.

After the meal, Noah picked up his daughter and danced with her slowly around the room. He did this by holding her to his chest while he spun slowly around the floor. Rutah loved the dance music and enjoyed herself immensely, but her little body began to tire out, making her yawn. Her father took her to their hotel suite were she fell fast asleep until the morning.

As for Noah, he was so proud of this precious gem. All he could do was to wait for his plans to go into effect. For now, he needed sleep also so that they could catch their flight back home.

More than two years past since Sylvia had seen Shane. In that interlude, she had the entire interior of the ranch house remodelled. She couldn't wait to see him again, show him the changes inside the house and renew their love lust. Slipping out to the car, Sylvia went to meet Shane at their usual hang out. Escaping her rodent of a child freed this woman to pursue her own fleshy desires.

After waiting a half hour, Shane never showed up. Disgruntled, Sylvia needed her instinctual desires met before going insane. Leaving the fast food joint, she walked to her car and drove an hour to *Boise*, *Idaho*. Here she searched downtown hunting for another young buck to satisfy her urges. She spotted a handsome nineteen-year-old lad working in the Kmart store. With a little feminine finesse, she had the lad's attention in no time flat and encouraged him to follow her to a spare change room at the back of the store.

Fifteen minutes later, they both walked out of the change room. As one at a time left the cubicle, they both pretended nothing ever happened. Thinking she had gotten away with it, Sylvia never suspected that a pair of dark brown eyes videotaped her quick escapade. Harry always tailed this slut wherever she went to catch her in any sex acts with other people. Then once a month, Harry would report to Noah with the results of his pornographic evidence.

= = =

When Rutah was five years old, Sylvia slithered off the ranch to find her tenth male of the week. Instead, she hooked up with her first (*but not last*) female sex partner. Harry managed to capture the whole event through an open bedroom window, were the curtains parted with enough space for the lens of the camera to poke inside the room, he got a clear shot of the events taking place.

During this interval, Noah summoned Rutah to his side and told her how much he loved her. However, that was not all, for the first time Noah told Rutah about how he was not her biological father. Yet he still loved her even more so, as if she was his only daughter.

Rutah may not have understood completely what her father had discussed with her; she somehow knew instinctively that GM was a wonderful person to have as her father. That's why she clung so tightly to him, since the age of two.

Sylvia's escapades continued until one late summer day a visitor came to the Nowhere Ranch door. When the house cleaner opened the front door, this man had arrived to surprise Sylvia. The house cleaner brought the man into the living room and asked him to wait. As he waited, he heard muffed female voices from the far bedroom. In one minute Sylvia walked around the corner of the hallway, stopped dead in her tracks and her mouth dropped down to the floor.

"Shane!" said the jovial woman. "Long time no see! Where have you been?" She walked towards him with her arms out stretched.

Hugging each other, Shane finally stated, "It's a long story!" Then he asked, "Can we visit so I can explain?"

"Sure let's have coffee and catch up on old times," stated the giggly Sylvia. She led Shane into the kitchen.

At one point during their conversation, Shane asked. "Did you have a boy or a girl while I was away?"

"I gave birth to a girl. We call her Rutah Allison Body," stated Sylvia coldly.

Time flew by as the two secret lovers continued talking. Eventually they both arranged to renew their former ways and made plans for the following week.

While Sylvia was catching up on old times with her former sexual partner in the ranch house, Noah and several ranch hands were busy that April morning, with a newly collected herd of wild mustangs.

The lead grey stallion was the last one left, but the energetic brute was not going to let any human predator tame him. For an hour, this steed would fight for the last stance and stood at times on his hind legs, kicking with his front ones. Other times he kicked wildly behind him trying to kill or severely injure any two-legged predators that approached too close. Two of the ranch hands had already received minor injuries. The rest were uncertain as to how they could get another lasso around the moving beast's neck.

As the stallion paced back and forth within the corral, little Rutah came to watch the cowhands at work. Standing on the bottom railing of the corral fence, she could observe the action going on between the gap of the top and middle railing. She saw that the horse had one rope around his neck, panted and pranced around the one side or the other. After ten minutes, Rutah called to her father.

"Papa, may I help?" she asked.

Noah turned to his daughter and put a reassuring arm around his daughter's shoulder. "And what can my little *Precious* do? That is a wild, scared and angry horse. What could you do to help? I think it might be too dangerous for you to enter the corral right now!"

With her insistent large eyes, Rutah pleaded, "Papa, I know I can help him. I want to help! Let me try to calm him down, please. **Please! Pleeeeeeease!** "

Rutah's pleas tugged at Noah's heart. How could he say '*no*' to his princess?

Against his better judgment, Noah finally ordered the other men to leave the corral. As they filed out, the stallion continued not to trust the humans on the outer side of the fencing.

The beast's pacing began to slow down and then stop. His nostrils continued to flare in and out, showing his anxiety and fury.

"Ok *Puddin'*. He's all yours! What are you going to do next?" queried her father.

All of the ranch hands waited anxiously to see what the little five year old could do that the older men couldn't.

With a twinkle in her eye, Rutah said, "I'll show you!" She then got off the railing and slowly walked toward the corral gate.

One of the older ranch hands, named **Geoffrey Stars**, bent over to Rutah's ear and said, "Are you sure you want to go in there?"

"Yes!" was her response.

"Well, in that case. If you need help, I'll be right here for you. Just call for me - Ok?" declared Geoffrey.

"Ok. But I think I may not need your help." Turning to Geoffrey with confidence, she smiled charmingly and said with a twinkle in her eye, "I think I can calm him down. Just watch!"

The tension around the corral fence was very high after the gate closed. Rutah ignored the others and kept her focus on the stallion. She slowly walked to the centre of the corral and faced the beast with a calm demeanour.

The steed didn't know what to make of this small female human. He still slowly paced back and forth with the rope around his neck, circling her couple of times, and keeping his suspicious eyes on her. When Rutah didn't move, the steed stopped pacing and finally began sizing her up. No doubt he was wondering what this little girl would do next.

Moving with extreme slowness, Rutah reached into her coat pocket and pulled out a large juicy red apple. With a slow movement, she extended her left arm out in front of her, showing the rich reward for the grey stallion. "This is for you, if you will become my friend" she exclaimed.

All the steed did was snort disapprovingly, but he was curious as to what she held out to him.

"She's cheating," whispered one of the cowhands.

"Don't complain," whispered Geoffrey, "If this works, then maybe she could teach us a few things about life." GM smiled at the men, while watching his daughter's technique.

Rutah's little arm started to ache as she tried desperately to keep the apple up in the air. Eventually she lowered her arm and brought the apple up to her mouth. Taking a crunchy big bite out of the apple, she made an approving sound of enjoying the fruit. Slowly chewing on the apple, she again extended her left arm up to the wild thing. "Mmm - it's good and juicy!" she declared, waiting to see how he would respond.

Shane finally pulled out of the driveway and left Sylvia watching him go while feeling young again. Waving goodbye as he drove off, she stood in the same spot looking longingly to their next liaison. Dazed for five minutes in her dream world, her peripheral vision alerted her that the work hands were just standing around the corral. Her blood pressure shot up and she went over to order the men back to work.

Still suspicious of Rutah's actions, the steed could sense that this little girl didn't mean to hurt him. Actually, she was trying to share some food with him. He was definitely hungry after all the action that morning. Before he moved, he eyed the taller humans to see what they were doing. Since they were not going to do anything, he slowly moved forward and sniffed the object in her hand. It sure smelt good. Therefore, he took a nibble and found it very sweet indeed.

Sylvia was halfway across the yard when she saw *Henrietta*, Rutah's favourite hen.

"I think we should have you for dinner, you flea infested large ball of feathers." Sylvia hated all of Rutah's pets and was determined to kill this one also. Grabbing the axe on the chopping block, Sylvia tried reaching down to grab the hen and cut off its head. Henrietta sensed the danger and zipped off at a great run, avoiding Sylvia like the plague.

"Stand still so I can catch you – you two legged lunch bucket," demanded Sylvia taking up the chase.

Henrietta squawked and flapped her wings, zigzagging all over the large yard. The only people who noticed the ruckus in the yard were the house cleaners and the chef. Shaking their heads in disgust, they waited to see if Sylvia would catch Henrietta this time around.

Sylvia was in hot pursuit until she slipped; face first; into a wet mud puddle, losing the axe in the process. The house cleaners and the chef laughed at Sylvia's failure before going back to their duties.

At this point, the hen shot off toward the corral seeking safety from Sylvia's clutches. As for Sylvia, she just growled under her breath and tried her best to stand on two slippery feet again. Finding the axe, she returned it to its chopping block on the other side of the yard.

"Just you wait you butter ball. I'll get you one day! When you least expect it, I'll get you! Just you wait and see," scowled Sylvia.

Rutah just smiled and let the stallion consume the entire apple in her open palm. After he was finished, she spoke in low reassuring words to him, "That was wonderful - wasn't it? Would you like more of them? I can get you more!" Then she slowly began to stroke his large muscular neck, while the tension around the corral dissipated into shocked disbelief.

It was at this moment that Henrietta slowed down to a trot and headed to Rutah's side from under the corral railing. To everyone's surprise, Henrietta's clucking and squawking seemed to calm the steed down even more. The hen moved around the front of the giant horse beast as if declaring she won the chase game, while she kept an eye out for Sylvia and that terrifying axe.

Rutah turned her attention to the bird, "Why Henrietta, are you going to welcome our new guest?" Bending down, she picked up the hen and held her gently before the stallion.

"Henrietta, I'd love you to meet our new friend, **Stanley**. Stanley, this is Henrietta." The horse and the bird seemed to greet and acknowledge each other in their own way.

"Well I'll be…," declared Geoffrey to Noah. "I'd never thought such a thing was possible! That both your daughter and a chicken could calm down such a wild beast."

Noah just smiled and patted Geoffrey on the back. "I think both girls used their feminine charms on the young lad and it worked. Rutah's one smart cookie when it comes to animals. Come on let's open the corral gate and take the wild beast to his new stall."

Rutah was holding Henrietta under one arm, while leading Stanley by the rope with the other hand. Everyone slowly gathered around Rutah and the men were astonished at how she could handle such a wild horse better than any of them could.

"I like to call him Stanley. Could I keep him for a while? I'll take good care of him!" declared Rutah.

"You bet you can *Pumpkin*. Go ahead and find a stall in the barn for him," stated her proud dad. "I'm sure there is a spot for him!"

Holding her head high and smiling back at everyone, Rutah led Stanley to the barn.

A round of light applause and gentle cheers went out to Rutah and Henrietta. It was at this point that Sylvia stormed over, covered in mud, to see what all the fuss and noise was about.

"**What's going on?** Why aren't these lazy bones working? Maybe you should fire them for not doing their duties?" fumed Sylvia.

When all the cowhands saw Sylvia with mud on her, they started giggling. Most of Noah's staff hated Sylvia for her cruelty to them, especially her yelling fits towards Rutah. To these people, Rutah was like a sweet little niece to them and they would gladly protect this beauty from <u>any</u> beast, especially her monstrous mother. Yet seeing this woman in her present state, all the cowhands could do, was enjoy her muddy misery.

Noah groaned and just rolled his eyes in to his head. Turning to Geoffrey, Noah winked and quietly said, "Get everyone back to their duties and help Rutah find a big stall for Stanley. I'll take care of this wench - personally!" Geoffrey nodded with a smile and went to assist Rutah by opening the barn doors wider. Noah returned his attention to the advancing *Nuisance*.

Facing Noah, Sylvia repeatedly poked a finger into his chest and continued her orders, "Am I not in charge here? Well answer me! On the other hand, should I just give everyone his or her severance pay? Quit fooling around and get these lazy bums back to work!"

"**Who's in charge**? **You demand what**! Severance pay for these hard working people! I'll demonstrate to you how to give someone **severance pay**," he declared with volcanic fury. Noah then quickly bent over, picked up Sylvia by her lower legs so her body flopped over his shoulder, and marched her off to the ranch house to the cheers, hoots and laughter of all the cowhands.

"Put me down - **you *reject*.** I demand you put me down! Are you deaf? I said let me down! Let go of me you ***Retard***! You hear me! **I order you to let go of me!**"

"You're not the one in charge, **I am**! You just get your useless ass back to your own business and let me do mine without your interference," continued Noah as he stormed off.

"Put me down you ***moron***. Only a mentally disturbed individual like you would pull off a stunt like this. I demand you put me down – **now!**"

Noah stopped in front of the mud puddle. "Right this minute?" he asked sarcastically.

"Yes - you *Asshole*!" shouted Sylvia.

"As you wish, *Sweet-fart,*" Noah continued his sarcasm. Then with a quick thrust, Noah managed to stand Sylvia up on her feet in one swift movement. Then he pushed her backwards, with great enthusiasm, into the same mud puddle she slipped into earlier.

All the cowhands who were on their way to do their duties saw her go down, roared with more laughter than before. The men raised cheers and applauses for Noah. Turning quickly to his men, Noah smiled and took a bow. Then he turned his attention back on Sylvia, with a scowl.

Like a kick in the teeth, Sylvia couldn't believe Noah would do such a rotten thing to her, especially in front of the hired hands. She was so upset; she began fuming, with tears rolling down her muddy cheeks. Next, she stood up on shaky, slippery legs to give him more of her verbal abuse while mud and water dripped off the back of her overalls. However, Noah beat her to the punch and bending over again, he grabbed her lower legs again to carry the mud soaked woman to the ranch house.

Flabbergasted at Noah's swiftness, Sylvia continued her protests all the way, until Noah yelled at her to shut her yap! Feeling she had lost all control of the situation, tears of frustration flowed from her eyes.

As soon as he got her to the kitchen door, Noah set her down, opened the door and pushed the now crying woman into the house. Slamming the door behind her, he brushed his hands clean, spun around and stormed off with a release of air from his lungs.

"Damn, that felt good!"

= = =

As time passed, Stanley became Rutah's close companion of five years before she sold him. From his loins came many young colts, each trained by the hired hands before they sold to prospective buyers around the country.

In the meantime, Henrietta, when alive, preferred to sleep in Stanley's stall, clucking her conversations to him and keeping this giant, relaxed. Some of her offspring later replaced this valuable bird to the sixth generation.

As for Noah, when not selling or buying equines, he made time for several stage productions with his friend Jay and The Red Bluff Players. As a result, he developed excellent acting and make-up techniques from the various parts he played. Whether the character was a gumshoe or a vagabond, Noah knew how to role-play his characters to realism. Some of his cowhands and house servants assisted on the stage productions. They even had bit parts.

In the meantime, some of Noah's friends encouraged him to split with Sylvia, take the money, Rutah and run for the hills. Nevertheless, in order for GM's plan to succeed, he needed to savour the waiting until Rutah was eighteen. This made it fun for him to keep Sylvia on his tight leash and choker, while allowing her to think she was the successful one.

As for Sylvia, she did one of several things. Spend money on renovations every four to five years or splurge on various cloths and accessories. Money just slid threw her fingers like water, but she found that she had to plan her spending sprees due to Noah tight grip on the funds.

The second thing she did was join The Red Bluff productions, on three different performances, with an air of finesse. Sometimes she took on the role of production manager and promoter, to the groans of the other players. Every time she was in charge, the production did lousy at the box office.

If she was not busy with the stage plays, then the third thing she did was being in charge of the women's club. With this event Sylvia could rendezvous with Shane about every two months or so.

Sylvia was not in a rush to get all of the ten million dollars from Noah, she just savoured the waiting in order to pounce on him when the time was right later on. Since Noah only allowed her an allowance each year, she masterminded a way to bide her time by slowly draining away the funds in the joint account.

## CHAPTER 10

# In the Left Pocket

By the age of seven, Rutah was developing into a beautiful youthful girl. Because of her beauty and energetic zeal for life, she was in one terrifying quandary, which shook her life. Because of this incident, her father developed a new silent way in which they could communicate with one another without Sylvia sticking her nose into their private conversations.

It happened one Saturday evening in June as follows...

In order to get a good start on their riding day, Rutah and her three school friends all went to bed early that Friday evening. Their enthusiasm for their outing was contagious. Although it sounded like a lot of fun to the place the girls were going to go, many hidden dangers existed. Therefore, to give the girls security and safety, two adults joined them. Uncle Geoffrey and Auntie *Mildred* (*the head house cleaner*) gladly came along to make sure everyone was safe. Geoffrey carried a shotgun to scare off any predators that would enjoy snacking on any cute girls.

Their little trip started from the ranch to *Tubular Dome* about four miles west.

This Dome was made of black compact granite. This name fit perfectly because the inside of this ancient volcanic tube resembled that of a piece of hollow straw sticking out of the ground. Inside of this straw was a cathedral-like chamber three hundred feet in diameter. By entering a small, six-foot high tunnel, on the east side of this mountain, a person dropped down a walkway slope at a 22-degree angle. After twenty-five feet, one would arrive at the floor basin of the cathedral chamber.

Geoffrey asked if the girls wanted to see inside the Dome. They all agreed! Taking the lead, Geoffrey led the girls into the chamber, while Mildred took up the rear guard. Once inside, no one needed a flashlight since the top of the Dome was open to the sky above. Like a black mirror, the granite had a way of refracting the light from above to the chamber below. The girls found it a fascinating location. On all the inner walls were various pictographs, either chiselled or painted on. Scattered around the ground were various types of bones, clay pottery (*some pieces broken*) and in the centre of the chamber looked like an ancient fire pit.

"Many Native Americans who traveled over the years must have used this spot for a sleep over," declared the amazed Mildred.

"They sure did!" agreed Geoffrey still looking around. "It's obvious by the pottery, bones and fire pit; they must have come through and spent a night or more here. Later cowpokes also used these caves from time to time during long cattle drives."

After a half hour, the girls wanted to go to the family swimming hole.

Turning north from the Dome, for half a mile, the girls would enjoy their swim and afternoon picnic on **Shallow Lake**. Auntie Mildred set up the picnic, while Geoffrey took care of the horses and then scouted out the area for danger. If any cougars or bears came around looking for food, he'd scare them off with the shotgun. The coast was clear, this time around!

Shallow Lake was so name because this patch of clear blue-green water, about a hector in circumference; was the result of the last glacier melt. Because the lake only reached to a depth of eleven feet, it was always warm by the direct sunlight and a favourite swimming hole of the family and staff. On the southern side of this lake was a small sandy beach about thirty feet long and two feet wide. Here is where Mildred set up the picnic basket and refreshments on a huge, flat slab of black granite. Buried at the right depth in the ground, this granite slab acted as either a table or humongous bench.

The girls felt cooled down from the hot day after a couple of hours of swimming. Then drying off from their swim, they ate a hearty lunch with the adults, before their ride back to the ranch.

As a surprise for all, Noah had planned a wild ranch barbeque with plenty of food and dancing. It was Noah's way of thanking all his employees for their hard efforts throughout the year. Of course, the girls would join in on this party as well!

To add more fun to the feast, he hired a local Custard band; called the **Hick Town Trumpeters**, to play various music pieces. The band consisted of two fiddlers, a flute player, a banjo player, two guitarists, a Jews harp player, a couple of jug blowers, a single stringed instrument (*looking like an upside down washing tub with a stick and string coming out of the bottom*) and an accordionist. They mostly played country and blue music, with a few waltzes and square dances thrown in.

During the dancing, the men; including Noah; allowed the girls to stand on their feet while they danced around. Great laughter and joy bounded by everyone, except the sour puss – Sylvia. She just stayed inside the house and refused to join in on the fun. She just sulked away because she had lost another fight earlier that morning with Noah. Therefore, instead of joining everyone else, she hid away, scheming out another plan to get Noah's cash. Little did she realize that a minute possibility was about to unfold in her lap that evening!

When the girls were tired, they were all ready for bed. Before they went to sleep, the girls thanked everyone for the food, music, dancing and making it a memorable time for them.

All the cowhands thanked the young people for the opportunity to take turns dancing with each of them (*even though they just stood on the men's feet in order to dance*). It was truly a memorable time for all, until …

While the music played, no one saw Shane drive up into the yard around 10:30 pm or bump his car fender into an old post. He was drunker than a skunk and reeked like one too. Fired from his job, Shane was seeking female companionship. Thinking he was in the clear without Noah around, he staggered over to the kitchen door, entered with some difficulty, in order to ferret out Sylvia. Once inside he tried to find his way to her bedroom, while few lights were on in the house.

He almost tripped down the living room step before he hit a footstool with his left foot. Tumbling down face first, he laughed and then shushed himself before standing again. When he got up, his head swirled in confusion. Yet he was determined to find Sylvia. He strutted slovenly forward toward the hallway.

When Shane rounded the corner of the hallway, was the same moment the girls were entering the living room from the patio doors. Yawning and eager to get to sleep, they all headed to Rutah's bedroom (*the spare bedroom farthest from her mother's master bedroom*).

Shane didn't notice or hear the girls come in. He staggered down the hallway and entered the bedroom closest to the laundry room. It was nothing but a spare bedroom. Upon entering, he found an empty bed, chest of drawers and a closet. He stood there swaying, trying to get his brain wrapped around his bearings. *Where am I? Why am I in here?*

The girls closed Rutah's bedroom door and changed into their sleepwear, unaware a drunken prowler was inside the house. They all climbed into their beds and fell fast asleep.

"Oh yeah, I'm here to see Sylvia," Shane slurred to himself.

Turning around he walked into the hallway and careened into the wall opposite the spare bedroom.

Sylvia was crying to herself at this episode, wallowing in self-pity, when she thought she heard a dull thudding sound against the far wall. She wiped away her watery eyes and runny nose. Slowly she got out of bed and walked to the bedroom door to see what caused the noise.

Turned around, Shane pitched forward, with a slight jog, into the laundry room.

Sylvia had just opened her door a moment after Shane disappeared into the laundry room. Looking down the hallway, she saw and heard nothing. If she had turned toward the laundry room, she would have seen Shane standing there with his back to her. Instead, she shrugged her shoulders and re-closed her bedroom door, not noticing Shane.

Noah thanked all of his staff for their co-operation and for making it a fun time for all the girls. He assisted with the clean-up, said goodnights to everyone and then headed to his bedroom opposite Sylvia's room for some sleep.

Once in the laundry room, Shane did not comprehend where he was until a bedroom light illuminated the interior of the room. Undulating again, he stood there trying to figure out where Sylvia was hiding. *This isn't her bedroom*, he thought before the light went out. He turned again to weave down the hallway.

Going too far down the hallway, Shane opened the door to Rutah's bedroom. He swung into the room quietly to size up the situation. With a small night-light illuminating the room, he could see eight, no, four bodies sleeping. Two female figures were in bunk beds while two others were in a double bed. *This is confusing*, thought Shane, *since when are there four Sylvia. Wait a minute, only one is Sylvia and the others must be her friends*, Shane concluded in his cloudy mind. *I'll find her;* he declared and he moved in like a swift silent predator.

Noah had just entered the house and kicked off his shoes when the screams came. Noah realized it was Rutah's voice and tore off to his daughter's room at a full sprint.

Sylvia heard the screams and went to investigate also, but at a much slower pace than Noah did.

Both parents arrived to find Shane lying on the floor, trying to protect himself. Two of the girls were screaming at this intruder and then grabbing anything they could, began beating the stranger into submission. Rutah was cowering in the corner of the double bed crying hysterically, while her other friend, *Tanya Hemp*, tried to comfort her.

Noah called a stop their attack, "**All right!** That's enough. **Stop it! That's enough!**"

When the girls stopped their attack on the intruder, Noah continued, "What's going on here? What happened?"

Rutah ran to her father and grabbed hold of him, violently trembling. She tried to talk through her sobbing, "he…touched me Papa. It was…was not pleasant."

Getting the girls to leave the area right away and sleep with the house cleaners in the staff quarters, Noah turned his beastly fury on Shane for the first time. Sylvia giggled to herself as the girls passed him by, thinking how ironic and idiotic Shane appeared.

The girls ran out of the house in hysterics and headed towards the staff quarters. Upon arrival, they frantically banged on the door to get in. Quickly Mildred, who was reading at the time, jumped out of bed and ran to open the door. She was astounded to see four panicked girls standing in the doorway, shivering as if cold and in terrifying tears.

"Come in quickly," she coached the girls inside.

As for Geoffrey, he was just locking down the barn doors, when he spotted, out of the corner of his eye, the girls' frantic dash to the staff quarters, from the ranch house. Instinctively he knew something was definitely out of place. He trotted to the door behind the girls to find out what scared them so badly. When he arrived, he followed the girls inside.

"What happened to you dears?" questioned Geoffrey with deep concern.

As the girls huddled together, they told both adults about how a stranger entered Rutah's bedroom and attacked Rutah while they slept.

By now the rest of the staff were up and listening to the girl's story. The confusion from the described event hit every adult with a jolt!

Geoffrey bent down on one knee and addressed all of the girls. Speaking in a low, calm voice, he said, "Listen to me. I know all of us agree that this bad man needs to be dealt with, right?"

The girls were calming down and shook their heads in agreement. Sniffling Rutah piped up, "Uncle? Please don't kill the man? Just get rid of him for me – Ok?"

"Sure thing *Princess*. Sure thing," stated Geoffrey as he gave Rutah a reassuring hug. As he finally let her go, he continued, "Now you beauties don't worry. Me and the boys will go and protect you darlings from this intruder."

As he stood up, he turned to Mildred, with a more serious tone, "Mildred, do you and the other women have enough room for the girls? If not, all of us guys will sacrifice our beds to accommodate them by sleeping in the barn loft!" All the men agreed whole-heartedly.

"I think we have more than enough room!" declared Mildred.

"Ok then," said Geoffrey.

Turning to the other men, "Boys let's get this demon off of our boss's property - Now!"

Leaving rapidly out the staff door, the men headed to the house at a full gallop.

"I can explain every...," Shane declared in a drunken tone. He never finished the sentence. Noah ploughed him one square punch in the nose, breaking it in the process and knocking him to the floor.

Turning to Sylvia and demanding, "**Did you know he was here?**"

"No I didn't know he was here!" stated Sylvia frankly, while crossing her arms.

"So why are you here – **you pervert!**" demanded Noah.

Blood poured out of Shane's nose; he tried to get up but was having difficulty doing so.

"**Well answer me?** Why are you here?"

Shane squeaked out, "to...to see...to see Sylvia!"

Sylvia rolled her eyes into her head. *Shane - you frigging bastard, how dare you confess our intimate rendezvous! You were to keep quiet about it. Noah doesn't know about us!*

"Why are you here to see my wife? Huh? **Answer me?**" demanded Noah, as he kicked Shane in the shin.

"Ow! I just...I just... wanted to talk to an old friend. That's all... nothing... more!"

"Couldn't it have waited until morning? Or was your idea of hitting on our daughter in the program?"

"I'm sorry… I didn't know I was in her room. Honest…I thought it was …"

Sylvia, gesturing with waving arms, cut Shane off before he spilled the beans, "So you enter Rutah's bedroom to talk to me. That's a lark if I've ever heard one! "

"Oh shut up Bitch!" fumed Noah. "He enters our home and attacked our daughter, thinking he has the right to this place any old time he wishes. Nice try! He was here hoping to have a romp with you. Is that it? That's quite a joke, since your married to me."

"Maybe the joke should have been him having a roll in the hay with Rutah. It would do her much good! Besides she is your biological daughter, **not mine**." Spinning on her heels, she stomped down the hallway, slamming her bedroom door in the process.

By this time, several of the cowhands raced into the home to help Noah after hearing what happened to Rutah. Seeing Noah had everything under control, they waited to have their turn to deal with Shane personally, for hurting their favourite niece and scaring her school friends.

"As for you," sternly warned GM to Shane, "You are never to come near the Nowhere Ranch again, unless I personally invite you. **Is that understood?**"

"Yes, I understand," Shane complied after getting up on his wobbly legs. The blood from his nose had stopped flowing. "I'm sorry! I'm truly sorry for disrupting everyone. Can't you find it in your heart too…?"

Turning to his ranch hands, Noah stated with great rage, "Get this piece of shit out of my house! **Now!** Before I beat him into road kill."

Geoffrey said, "With pleasure boss, with pleasure! Come on vermin, get a move on!" Grabbing Shane by the scruff of the neck, Geoffrey dragged the drunk to his car.

Noah sat down on Rutah's bed to calm down his nerves and defuse his rage. Rubbing his forehead and then his neck, he used various breathing techniques to relax his nerves. Then a thought entered into his mind. It was something Sylvia said. Getting up he went to address her lousy attitude.

As soon as the boys had Shane outside, they began beating on him so that he would be black and blue all over his body the next morning. Then they tossed him into his car and ordered him to drive home and never come back. With such fearful adrenaline racing through his body, Shane spun his car around on the gravel lot and fled the ranch at top speed.

"What a jerk! How could he do a rotten thing to our beautiful niece?" asked *Job Floors*.

"Some people never learn Job. Some men think that everything in life is a game, including sexually assaulting young children," stated Geoffrey.

"The next time he comes here, how about we castrate that bastard?" asked *Wyatt Bench*, the younger ranch hand.

"We'll have to see what the boss says about that subject," said Geoffrey. He then continued, "But if you are asking me, personally. I think more than castration should be done to the asshole." Turning his attention to the others, "Let's see how our girls are doing, Ok boys?"

All the men nodded in agreement. They slowly sauntered to the staff quarters.

Noah went to talk to Sylvia, but she refused to discuss anything with the *Reject*.

"What the hell is your problem? Your daughter was molested this evening and you sit here refusing to discuss the situation?" Noah asked fumingly.

"Like I already said, she is your daughter, not mine!"

"How can you make such a claim? You don't do anything with her. You just spend most of your time insulting and putting her down. You kill her pets and destroy her school artwork. Remember, she is part of your genetic code. By insulting her, you are also are insulting yourself!"

"So - who cares? She is your useless problem not mine. Besides, if Shane wants to poke his nose around here, let him. All this does is drive you nuts, doesn't it *Moron*?" *Man, do I enjoy every minute of this*, she thought to herself. She continued her aggressiveness, "You're a useless and stupid man, *Reject*! You never get anything right, *Idiot*." Her voice rose even louder to him, "You're such a loser and failure of society! You don't even know how to raise a child properly, *Retard*. Anything that can…"

A loud '*Smack*' sound reverberated around the room.

For the second time that evening, Noah exploded in a Krakatoan rage. In one quick movement, he backhanded Sylvia hard across her right cheek. The force of this action sent her flying across the bedroom, landing on top of her bed sideways. Looking back at her assailant, loose hair strands fell across her ever-reddening cheek. With anticipation for this outburst on his part, she focused her full attention on Noah and challengingly said, "So that's your game, eh? Hit me will you?" She continued to egg GM on, "Try it again and I will sue you for every penny you have. Hear me! Come on! Just try it again, *Asshole*! **COME ON!**"

Noah stopped dead in his tracks. *She is right*, he thought. She bated him into hitting her and thus giving her the control she wanted, the threatening ability to confiscate everything he owned, including his money. He couldn't believe she sucked him into this provoked state of mind. His fierceness hadn't dissipated fully yet, so he stated flatly to her, "We'll see *Nemesis*! We'll see who wins this duel! Trust me; you're the loser and a failure in this round, **not me!**"

Laughing devilishly aloud at how she got him good, she jumped off the bed to face him and continued her verbal onslaught by increasing her volume. As spittle flew from her mouth, she used stabbing poison-tipped words at GM.

Refusing any longer to play into her childish showdown, Noah pirouetted on his heels and proceeded to leave this menace's torture chamber.

Beaming with profound glee, she continued to voice her assault by trying to goad GM into action that is more violent.

Ignoring her, Noah slammed the door on the way out. The force from the door caused some pictures on each side of the walls to bounce around and tilt sideways.

She was thrilled to death at gaining some of her power back. Roaring with vicious enthusiasm, she mused, *what a masterful manoeuvre on my part*. Only this was a short-lived victory for her!

Leaving the house, Noah went over to the staff quarters to see how his daughter and her friends were fairing. He met up with the men who also were concerned about Rutah and her friends. When he got there, Mildred told all the men that the girls finally calmed down and fell asleep. Wyatt asked that they keep an eye on the girls throughout the night, even if they took turns doing it. If anything was wrong, they were to get hold of GM immediately, no matter what.

The cowhands offered to take turns guarding the Staff house in case that fool wanted to return. Noah thanked the men for their suggestion and allowed them to organize their own watch duties.

All who were not on duty went back to bed to sleep until called for.

Noah had a hard time sleeping that night. He went over to the hammock hanging in the porch area. Lying back on the swinging device, his mind raced through all possible questions and probabilities.

*How could this have happened to my daughter? Moreover, why was her mother so much against the girl? What was Shane's real purpose for being here...?*

With no satisfying answer, his sleepy eyes finally got the better of him.

When the sun began shining through the open fencing, it hit him directly in the eyes, startling him awake.

Rutah had a bad night's rest and so did her friends. She kept having nightmares about a shadowy figure chasing her and wanting to harm her. Several times, she woke up screaming and sweating profusely. Mildred did what she could to comfort this distraught one, until the girl calmed down. Eventually Rutah would go back to sleep, only to have another version of the same nightmare repeat again.

In the morning, with blood shot eyes, Rutah slumped out of bed to eat breakfast. Nevertheless, her tummy hurt so much from fear she couldn't eat.

Her friend's parents came over to pick up their children that morning and found out what Shane had done. Disbelief and astonishment ran through the parents. They knew it wasn't Noah's fault for what happened to his daughter. Although Noah told them, he had handled the problem and requested that the parents keep it to themselves; these adults could not keep quiet. In a matter of six hours, Shane Hunter's name was now mud in the town and community of Custard. A vigilante group was formed and they searched everywhere in town, hunting down this assumed pedophile.

As for Shane, he had already fled from the area before anything more could happen to him. His puffed-up face and black and blue marked body showed where every blow from the cowhands took its toll. He never came back to the area for the next eight years. By then the town's anger would have cooled off and everyone would have forgotten about him.

Sylvia went back to her selfish slump. Shane was gone, along with his masculine power and so were her dreams of beating Noah out of his millions. Instead, she retreated into her own little world and seemed to wilt away in a corner of the bedroom, very seldom coming out to eat or talk to anyone.

Rutah's fears from that event were not without substance. The previous evening set in motion a terrifying event in her life. In order to overcome it, she moved into the female staff quarters from that day forward.

As for the cowhands, they felt it was time to find a way to help their sweetheart sleep better at night. Every time Rutah screamed, it sent shock waves through their bodies and disrupted their caring hearts. Not one man could stand seeing their boss's daughter so hysterical and having a lousy nights rest.

Thinking for a while, Geoffrey was the one who came up with a possible solution. He went to his room and came out with a small, dark brown, homemade, patchwork teddy bear. It had a light blue ribbon around its neck with a hand-sewn name on it, **Ben**. Uncle Geoffrey told Rutah to hold onto this special bear. When he was her age, he had bad dreams too. However, when he held Ben in his arms, it seemed like Ben entered his dreams and chased away the monsters. After the monsters were gone, immediately the bad dreams disappeared – never to return.

Although smart, curious but sceptical, Rutah asked her uncle, "Where did you get such a special bear from?"

"My sister made it for me when I was five years old. I hung onto that bear every night for dear life because of my scary dreams. Then one night, I had a dream in which Ben came to my rescue. After he chased away the monsters, he told me to no longer worry because from then on my dreams would be good ones."

"Were they good ones?" asked Rutah.

"They sure were. I never had a scary nightmare like that again," reassured Geoffrey.

"Wow!" expressed Rutah.

"That's why I want you to sleep with him tonight and see if he helps you get rid of your nightmares too," stated Geoffrey.

*If Ben helped Uncle Geoffrey, maybe he could help me too*, reasoned Rutah. Then a thought struck her, "How old was your sister when she made Ben for you?"

"She was nine years old at the time. But she passed away a year after making Ben."

"Oh! I'm sorry to hear that," pouted Rutah. "What did she die of?"

"That's ok *Sweet Pea*. She died of double pneumonia. At that time, the doctors did not have a cure or any medicine to help her with this disease. Today, she lives on in my memories. I loved my sister and I know she loved me."

"How do you know she loved you?" enquired Rutah.

"Even though I came from a poor family, my sister scrounged up the materials necessary to make Ben for me. That's how I know."

"Oh!" said Rutah. Giving her uncle Geoffrey a big hug, she said, "Thank you for lending Ben to me. I'll sleep with him tonight and see if the bad dreams will stop."

"I know they will sooner or later. I just know they will," reassured the smiling Geoffrey.

After a bad week of sleep, Rutah finally had an unusual dream were Ben appeared. Speaking in her father's voice, he told Rutah to wait and see what happens.

In her dream, the shadowy figure with claws and long fangs began to form into a deformed Shane. Shane was ready to attack her. Instead of coming at her like all the other evenings,

Ben appeared and came to her rescue. Growing ten times larger than Shane does, Ben chased him away, permanently.

Rutah hugged Ben in her dream and thanked him for helping her. Nevertheless, Ben told her that she was now a big enough woman to defend herself from all her future monsters.

Before the dream ended, Ben bent over and picked a wild flower for Rutah. He told her to keep it close to her heart and all would be well.

When Rutah awoke, it was the first time in a week she woke up refreshed and happy again. She hunted down Uncle Geoffrey to give Ben back to him. She thanked him for the use of Ben and told him about the dream. Geoffrey gave Rutah a hug and told her that he was certain that Ben would show up to help her. Both of them laughed.

It was that morning that Noah called Rutah to join him in a walk. While walking together, her father came up with the idea of using a flower; any type of flower; either taped, pinned or put into the left breast pocket or left coat lapel. By doing this, it was a silent way of communicating that Rutah or her father wanted to talk to the other person, without Sylvia interfering. Both of them would meet over at the top of Seven Mile Hill, as soon as possible. Rutah loved the suggestion! From that day forward, they always implemented this covert communication between themselves.

= = =

By the time, Rutah was thirteen; many changes took place in the horse industry as well as the ranch life.

Phases had become easier after the 1989 to 1991 stock market slump. Some businesses that had closed their doors during this rough cycle, tried to make a comeback. Noah also struggled during the same tough times, but he refused to eliminate any staff members or allow a temporary setback to stop his operations. He kept them going while his bank account dropped to forty three million dollars.

Although disasters strike people at different intervals, this Body family was no exception to the rule. Noah had just finished talking to his mother two days before her death in 1993. He found out from his older brother Calvin that his mother died suddenly of a brain haemorrhage, during the night of August 1st. Noah was devastated and he wore a flower to get Rutah's attention.

When Rutah got home from her swim at the swimming hole, she saw the flower in her father's pocket and his depressed look. She knew something terrible had happened. They both traveled to Seven Mile Hill together before speaking to each other.

When her father parked the truck, he said, "I have some bad news to share with you. Would you come with me as we walk down to the meadow overlooking the Sunshine Valley?"

"Of course Papa, let's go," said the concerned Rutah.

Once they got to their favourite spot in the meadow, Noah turned to Rutah and said, "Puddin', your Uncle Calvin called me earlier today. He let me know that Grandma had passed away suddenly last night."

"Oh no!" exclaimed Rutah at this disturbing news. "What happened?" she asked frowning, while reaching out to her father. Rutah loved her grandmother as much as she loved her father.

"Granma had a Brain Haemorrhage and it killed her quickly," said the teary-eyed Noah.

"Oh Papa!" exclaimed Rutah. "I'm so sorry to hear such sad news!" Tears started streaming down her cheeks as she grabbing hold of her father, hugging him tightly.

"I know Puddin', I know" Noah cried also, hugging Rutah tightly.

Through their sobs, Rutah asked when her funeral would be. Noah was not sure at the time but his brother would notify him later about it.

After their crying together for some time, both parties dried their eyes and watched the setting sun. Then they both took turns reminiscing about Connie. There were more fond memories about her than sad ones.

When the sky turned almost blood red, both of them went back to the truck and headed home.

This was not the only disaster to hit the Body household that year.

Geoffrey had married Mildred seven years earlier and they made quite a loving pair together on the ranch.

One month after Connie's funeral, Geoffrey and Wyatt were out scouting new territory for the horses to graze. While riding close to the Dome, a huge male Grizzly attacked them from the side, without warning.

The horses reared up sending both men to the ground, scampering off to the safety of the ranch.

Geoffrey didn't grab hold of his shotgun as he hit the ground, but Wyatt managed to do so.

The grizzly charged both men and knocked them over. Returning it proceeded to maul Geoffrey. Wyatt was able to get to his feet, aim and fire the gun. It took three shots to kill the beast as it turned and charged toward him.

When Wyatt reached Geoffrey's side, Geoffrey's wounds were so severe that he slowly bled to death. The only words he got out were, "Tell Mildred I love her. Please, tell her I love her!" Then Geoffrey expired!

Wyatt couldn't do a thing to stop the bleeding or Geoffrey's death. Leaving Geoffrey's body, Wyatt ran back to the ranch as fast as possible.

When the horses returned to the ranch without riders, Noah sensed something was wrong and amiss. Twenty minutes later Wyatt raced into the barnyard before a search party started.

Upon arriving back at the ranch, falling to the ground and out of breath, Wyatt eventually gasped out to Noah and the other men what had happened. They rode out quickly to retrieve Geoffrey's body before other predators could consume his remains. Wyatt sought Mildred to inform her of Geoffrey's final words to her. Then he retreated away, taking it very hard and blaming himself for Geoffrey's death.

At the funeral, Wyatt kept his blame game up not eating or sleeping very well. No matter how much comfort the staff given him or how much of a hero others told him he was for slaying the grizzly, Wyatt just spiralled deeper into his destructive depression. Eventually he left the Nowhere Ranch, never to return.

Mildred took her situation quite harshly at first. Over time, she accepted the loss of her beloved partner and moved on with living her life to the full.

Two days after the mauling incident, a mare escaped from her stall and bolted away from the ranch, opposite Seven Mile Hill. All of the cowhands followed on horseback, in hot pursuit, not long after. Since he had extra time on his hands, the chef tried to join in on this endeavour. He could only follow on foot. That's when the unthinkable happened!

While walking through the middle of a large mountain meadow, the chef was unaware of and caught off guard by a freak storm that hit his position swiftly. The dark thunderhead rolled in, distracting the chef's attention for a moment. Not watching where he stepped, his right foot sank into ankle deep mud patch beside a swamp. Trying hard to get his foot unstuck, the chef removed his apron, placed it on the ground beside him and yanked on his leg. Bent over and straining with all his might, the gumball mud refused to release his foot. He stood up at one point.

The cowhands found the mare three miles away, munching calmly on fresh sweet clover. Without any trouble, they were able to recapture her and return her home. Then they saw and later heard an overpowering lightning bolt strike the ground under the menacing thunderhead. Startled briefly by the flash of light, the horses became more agitated when the thunder roared a few seconds later. The cowhands calmed them all down and eventually were able to lead the animals homeward. After the quick three-minute shower burst, the thunderhead continued its antics, racing across the valley floor, to the hills on the other side. That's when the men came upon a gruesome sight. The chef's last stand was three quarters of a mile southwest of the ranch house. An intense bolt of lightning struck him there. All they found left of his remains was just a pile of ashes, a partially chard apron and his right foot stuck in the now hard baked mud.

Two fully paid for funerals, by Noah, in one week killed the joy of everyone on the Nowhere Ranch.

One more incident happened on the day of the funerals during the same stretch of time.

While everyone was at the two funerals, only Sylvia stayed home like the recluse she'd become. A loud knock came to the kitchen door. She slowly walked over to open the door. What an overwhelming sight she beheld before her very eyes.

After an eight-year absence, Shane showed up in Sylvia's life again. He had changed over the years. First thing was his comb-over look to cover the bald spot on his head. Next, he grew lamb-chop sideburns that blended in with his handlebar moustache. As for his jaw line, chin and under the neck, these areas were kept clean-shaven. He also added ten extra pounds of weight (*during the next two years, Shane gained an addition 30 pounds, before he started losing all that weight*).

"Sylvia, how are you?" asked the jubilant Shane.

"Shane? Where, the devil, have you been? What are you doing here? You do realize that the cowhands want to kill you if they see you here?" declared the astonished Sylvia.

Sylvia never comprehended how long she needed attention from Shane. She had lost a lot of weight over the years and she now look like skin on a skeletal structure. Without Shane's energy, she was gradually withering away and slowly dying inside. Now that he was back, she was renewing her desires for his company and couldn't wait to hit the sack.

"Come on lover boy!" she coached, with renewed vigour.

Off they went for a three-hour romp before the others returned. During their fun, Shane left a pair of his briefs with semen and bloodstains on them, under the corner of the bed.

When the time was up, Shane rapidly dressed, slipping out and promised to return. Sylvia suggested they meet at the old Gut Busters the next day and make their permanent plans from there.

Once Shane was gone, Sylvia was feeling reinvigorated. Her determination to get even with Noah began to grow again. She knew she had concealed three aces up her sleeve to defeat the *'Retard.'*

"Yes, I'll be getting you soon," she declared, "real soon!"

First, she had to gain more strength and weight to handle the future hurdles head on.

Therefore, she trotted off to the kitchen…

Noah came home without knowing Shane was back. Instead, he went to bug Sylvia that she missed two very good funerals. When Noah peeked into her bedroom, he found a messy room but no Sylvia. Therefore, he straightened her bed up, including the heavy down-filled comforter. That is when he noticed a pair of light blue men's briefs left on the floor under the corner of the bed. "Caught yah in your sex act *Madame Rambunctious*! Wait a minute! Whose are these? I wonder if these belong..." Shane's name was hand lettered on the inside of the waistband in black permanent ink. "So, he's back to wreak havoc on the family again," Noah fumed. "And he was just here a while ago!"

Examining the briefs better, Noah spotted the semen and blood stains on the fly area. "That confirms it. I'll get these tested and see if Shane maybe Rutah's true father or not." Finding a zip-lock bag in the kitchen drawer, Noah zipped the bag shut after dropping in the briefs. Next, he thoroughly cleansed his hands from any possible contamination from the briefs.

Contacting Harry by phone, Noah asked to see him right away. When Harry arrived at Sing Soot's Restaurant, Noah asked if Harry knew a lab that did genetic testing. Harry knew several labs and wanted to know what Noah wanted done. Noah looked around the room before handing over the evidence in the zip-lock bag.

"I want the semen and blood stains on these briefs tested for genetic material and have it compared to Rutah's DNA file. If Shane is her true father, I want to know these facts. Also, if there is anything else like, any diseases he may be carrying, I what that information as well. Can this be done?" queried GM.

"Now days, you bet it can. I'll get right on it as soon as possible," said Harry slipping the bag into his overcoat pocket.

"Good! Here is something extra for your trouble," stated GM. He slipped the detective a small envelope with twenty thousand dollars inside.

"Thank you," whispered Harry, sliding that into an inner pocket of his suit. "It's always a pleasure to do business with you sir!" smiled the gumshoe.

Mister Sing brought their meals to them with a smile. While they silently ate, GM's brain reminded him of his plans and that the time was right to implement each step.

First, he had to go to the only bank account Sylvia figured he owned. Although she never knew the exact amount hidden within his separate personal account, Noah would drain the joint account of all its funds. For his manoeuvre to work, the joint account they had been depleted in less than eight months.

In addition, Noah needed to retire from the equine industry. His famous breeding ranch, known throughout the United States for his exceptional strain of horses, seemed to be tiring him out. Nevertheless, the time would come for him to give up this pursuit and free himself from all worries. He would definitely make it well worth it for everyone employed, but this had to take place in the summer of 1997.

As for his daughter, she would be getting her Learner's Permit in a few months. Soon time would fly by and she would have her Driver's License, so GM needed to act rapidly on the layout to succeed in the final fight.

He had more steps to his scheme to complete. These plans would commence at the appropriate times he designated. Right now, the banking situation was of prime importance to initiate.

The next day, Shane met Sylvia at the designated locale. While deep in conversation as to what had happened to both of them over the years, Shane excluded telling one small piece of information to Sylvia.

Roughly two years before coming back to Custard, Shane met up with what he thought was a gorgeous female prostitute. In reality, it was a male transvestite, disguised as a female prostitute. Because he was drunk at the time, he didn't care what happened or what he did.

After he paid for the wild time with this prostitute, the prostitute congratulated Shane on joining his club. Before Shane could clue in about the comment mentioned, this male sex predator told Shane he had the AIDS virus and enjoyed giving it to him. Shane was devastated at such news. He never used any protection during his escapades with this cute female impostor. Now he received the same disgusting disease that destroyed such beauty.

After their sexual adventures the day before, Shane didn't use any protection. Sylvia never noticed that Shane wasn't using any either. Caught up in the experience of the moment, Sylvia constantly desiring the powerful orgasmic highs she received every time she was with Shane.

In the meantime, Sylvia sketched out several locations around Boise and Custard for them to implement their sexual capers without interruptions.

= = =

Two weeks later, Harry found Noah practicing a new stage play with The Red Bluff Players. Waiting for his cue to return on stage, Harry called Noah to come further away from the action and see what he brought him.

"The proof is in the pudding," Harry said flatly.

Noah opened the manila envelope and read the contents. Shane was definitely the father of Rutah. "This will definitely devastate my girl," Noah calmly told Harry.

"There's more!" Harry hinted at the other report, "Look at the next pages!"

Noah was startled at the report! Shane had the AIDS virus and his life span completely cut short in five more years or less.

"Good Lord above!" Noah exclaimed. He may have wanted to kill Shane at one time, but not like this. Then a thought hit him hard, *Sylvia had sex with this person just two weeks ago. Could she be carrying the AIDS virus too?*

"Harry, if I get another sample in the future, will you also test it for the AIDS virus?"

"No problems!" Harry continued, "Anything for you sir!"

"Good. As soon as I have it, I'll contact you, all right?" declared GM.

"Yes sir. I'll talk to you then!" said Harry.

Noah placed the information into his coat pocket and then his curtain call to be back on stage.

"I've got to go!" Noah walked on stage, reciting his lines from his well-rehearsed performance.

Turning quietly, Harry slipped stealthily out the back stage door unnoticed.

Noah recognized that evening after practice that he had to get a blood sample from Sylvia to screen her for the AIDS virus. If she, were infected, he would need to move in with Rutah and the staff. He also needed to have Rutah and his own blood tested for the same disease. Although he felt confident that the two of them were clean, he just had to make sure.

Once Noah had that information, he sat down with his family doctor to get more insights into the various diseases. When his doctor asked him why he needed such information, GM explained that The Red Bluff Players were performing a new play and he needed the information for research purposes.

# CHAPTER 11

# Let the Games Begin!

The year: 1998.

It had taken the Noah four years to get to this point.

The season: mid-summer.

One year had passed since the Game Master entered the old local Cypress Theatre just off Main Street. All of The Red Bluff Players were there, practicing the latest parts of their next stage production, *The Final Solution*.

Whenever GM showed up, the rehearsals would stop so all could have a break and catch up on the latest gossip, similar to a fifteen-minute break, only this break would sometimes take up to two hours to complete. Always glad to visit his comrades of the stage, Noah addressed the concerns and financial problems that the troupe faced. Their biggest concern was the Cypress itself. The situation was not because the theatre was over a hundred years of age. The fact was that someone with a lot of wealth had purchased it.

The Cypress was to be demolished within sixteen days, to make way for a new building complex. This made it harder for the troupe to continue their productions in such a classic theatre; especially when one knew she was to vanish forever. If they only had a benefactor to assist them out financially in the purchasing the building, they could keep the old theatre and continue their productions. At great cost, the aging building would need a complete overhaul. This would be to the tune of six hundred and seventy-five thousand dollars (*including the purchase price*).

Knowing their feelings about the problem, Noah sat poker faced while listening to everyone's concerns. Sometimes when the women cried about the theatre loss, he would comfort them by giving them a hug, while still listening to their concerns.

"If we could only talk to the new owner and explain our concerns to them, maybe they could leave the old theatre alone and build around it," exclaimed *Jane Bugle*.

"Yeah, right!" declared *Corky Snow*, "As if anyone would want to listen to our plea! This is the best place we've ever worked in."

"Where are we going to go then?" questioned *Jill Mainstream*, "The super market or the high school gym to put on our performances."

"Maybe," started GM with dramatic flair, "the solution to your dilemma is much easier than you think."

"What do you mean by that wise crack?" demanded Jay, "You know as much as we do that the theatre is the only place to perform our art!"

The others spoke in agreement with Jay.

"Besides," Jay continued with a suspicious look on his face, "you know something that you're not telling us! Am I right?

Come on GM, you know something and that is why you are here. So spit it out!"

Without saying a word, Noah looked at his friend's faces, one at a time and finally smiled when he hit the last face – Jay. "You're still on the ball aren't yah lad? I could never pull the wool over your eyes, could I?" questioned Noah. Jay smiled back to his best friend.

"Yes, I do know who purchased this building and I've talked to the person extensively about your plight. But be reassured that I know you'll want to hear what is going to happen to the Cypress."

No one spoke! They all just waited on GM to tell them what was going on.

"There is no way a person could repair the old theatre in its present state. The building is way too old and needs to be torn down."

Groans circulated around the room. Holding his hands up to silence the actors, Noah continued. "But if a new theatre were built upon the old buildings location, with the latest in engineering designs and improved acoustic capabilities, would anyone of you still want to object about these changes?"

No one said a word. Instead, they all looked at each other with puzzled expressions and then refocused their attention on Noah. For the first time in years, Noah felt the power of being on stage again, giving an authoritative speech to a captive audience. Revelling in this renewed power from his old experiences Noah continued his dialog.

Standing up and then pacing slowly around his friends, he explained that he was the one that bought the Cypress. His new theatre design would have more stage space, including a section of the stage jutting out into the audience for sixty feet.

The band pit would be a little deeper, giving more head room for the musicians and designed with the latest electronic microphone system so that even a single musician could be heard playing a musical piece loudly.

The balconies would surround the stage area (*including the walls*) in a semi-circular design. Even the acoustics of the building would improve that an actor could yell or whisper their lines and every audience member could hear them clearly. No muffled sounds of any kind, just crisp clear voices or music.

From the surrounding hallways around the main auditorium were various side rooms to accommodate all types of artisans and entertainers. Some of the eight largest rooms were for classes to educate people of all ages in various forms of art; for example: painting portraits, stills, clay work, various dance classes, music practicing rooms, etc. etc. Each room would be designed with a certain amount of sound proofing material so all students could enjoy their classes without any interruptions from other classrooms or even stage productions.

Six emergency exits, well-lit hallways and wall-mounted floor plans will assist people to find an escape route in case of a fire.

An enlarged parking lot provided the needed space to accommodate the necessary influx of people for performance nights.

When GM finally finished his powerful performance all looked at him with dazed looks. Then with great joy began to cheer and applaud their friend's new ideas. They were all happy to know that he was the one doing this project and not a complete stranger. They had to wait though to put on their performance and were not sure how to survive in the meantime.

Noah let them know that he needed their help on a problem he had. The event would require their full co-operation if his plan was to work flawlessly. In addition, the whole scheme needed execution within six days.

"This will be a tournament between the intellectual brainpower of a Mastermind versus a Game Master," he reminded them. Then he posed the following, "Who will succeed this task is the question which will soon be answered. Are you guy's game?"

Curious and excited to take on a new but temporary challenge, they all listened to the Game Master's plans. Noah laid out his plans with just enough detail to see if any of the troupes would refrain from helping or enthusiastically take it on.

No one objected.

Confident of their support, the Game Master offered wages to his friends to keep them going until the new Cypress Theatre Complex was finished.

However, that's not all!

Selecting seven of his closest friends (*two were women*) to one side, Noah arranged fees for their private services; fifty thousand dollars each; not just for their acting skills, but also for the use of any stage props, make-up, special effects and to bribe them for their silence.

Taken aback at such generous offers, those selected wanted more than ever to help their friend.

Leaving his comrades until needed, Noah took care of all deals the next morning. He also set up a fund in Jay's name, for the new Cypress Theatre complex.

*Buying such help was worth it*, thought Noah.

Noah went to his lawyer for all legal documents necessary for his next strategy of success to take place. He made sure he had everything in duplicate and ready to go. When the signing was complete, the papers returned to his attorney's office.

GM was now motivated more than ever.

He was ready to accomplish his most vital move ever, dealing with a pair of gold diggers! After which he would gain his freedom.

This will be a battle of brainpower between a Mastermind and a Game Master. Which one will be the winner?

To find out, GM declared in a loud voice, "Let the games begin!"

# CHAPTER 12

# KP - k4 or 25 - 45[6]

While sitting in the living room in his luxurious Nowhere Ranch, Mister N. O. Body had gathered everyone necessary for his master plan to begin. The following attended; his wife - **Sylvia**, his daughter - **Rutah**, a so-called friend - **Shane**, six well-dressed attorneys, and a mysteriously man called **Kelvin** (*he was Jay in disguise*). All were present as requested. Noah had the reputation as a skilled player of mind games and puzzles. That's why he was nicknamed *"The Game Master"* or *"GM"*, for short, by his friends.

The Game Master began his speech; "I've gathered everyone here today to clear the air once and for all!" His speech suddenly interrupted by a persistent cough. When Noah's throat cleared, he continued, "What I have to say will dumbfound, infuriate and distress any or all present. Therefore, here goes! Roughly, twenty years ago, a problem presented itself to me as a showdown. Since I've enjoyed games of challenge, like Chess, various board games, puzzles and

---

[6] You may never have seen this game move before. Therefore, check out the information in Appendix "E".

so on, this test of skill tweaked my intellectual powers." His coughing began again.

Rutah jumped up and spoke consolingly, "Papa, maybe it's better you sit down and...."

"No! *Puddin'*! I'll be fine" the GM waved his hand; just pausing to catch his breath. "It's just an annoying chest cold. That's all. I'll be fine," he said reassuringly to her. Sitting down again, Rutah waited to hear her father finish.

His spiteful wife Sylvia, bored already, sought an opportunity to attack her husband with her sly and cutting words. She seemed to coil up on the couch, like a serpent ready to strike against her victim. Her eyes narrowed viciously. *Patience*, she thought, *patience, savour the moment of when to strike. He's the one who's going to go down quickly. I'm the one with the three aces up my sleeve. I'm the mastermind, not HIM! I'm the winner of this competition, NOT HIM!*

After losing 5 pounds weight in the past month, Shane now whined, "Can we speed this process up? I've things to do and various place to go."

Rutah retorted, "As if that ever stopped you!"

Looking at Shane, Sylvia rebutted, "Shut up you *Whiner*. Let the *Retard* speak". Turning to her daughter, "**And you**, you ungrateful cow. *You* should show more respect towards your elders and no more sass from you!"

Rutah's eyes glared hatred back at her mother, but she finally relented to her mother's dominating stare and looked down to the floor.

The GM silently raised his hands to quiet all the combatants. "Please, please! I've got the floor, not any of you." The coughing started again.

Sylvia finally yelled, "Then get on with it - **MORON!** Your delay tactics and coughing will not work on us." Seething with venom, she felt justified in her first round of attack and smiled devilishly.

Rutah craned her gaze back to her father with loving concern. The coughing subsided. "**Fine,**" roared Noah, "Don't interrupt me! What I've got to share involves all of you." Pacing slowly and then pausing for emphasis, the Game Master let loose his first combative manoeuvre.

He addressed his wife, "You've been so spiteful towards me for the last eighteen years! Since you never slept at all with me since the time of our wedding night, you no doubt are scheming to have a divorce. **Correct?**"

Sylvia nodded with joyful contempt, "Of course you *Idiot*!"

Rutah thought to herself, while looking at her dad**,** *what are you up to - Papa?*

"Well then, don't worry; I've made the necessary arrangements for their preparation and for them to be signed, today! Are you game *Mastermind*?" he asked in a daring tone.

Smiling, Sylvia took up the challenge with eager enthusiasm, "Bring it on!" *I have you now,* she thought, *everything will be mine and you will get nothing. Not a damn thing! You'll be gone, without a single penny.*

Snapping his fingers, the first pair of attorneys presented the papers for signing. Upon receiving these documents, Sylvia glanced through the divorce papers. Meanwhile, unbeknown to the others, Kelvin (*Jay*) silently moved behind Sylvia by a cue from the Game Master. His stride was intensely slow and deliberate.

While going through the divorce papers, a copy of the special document, which she had signed unknowingly on their wedding day, slipped out from between some pages of the divorce papers. It landed onto the tabletop. Sylvia's devilish smile gradually diminished into a disappointing frown.

Picking up the special document, Sylvia couldn't believe GM had already out manoeuvred her to this point. Looking up, she barked, "What kind of garbage is this! **Are you insane? I'm not going to . . ."**

A metallic *'click'* sounded.

Sylvia froze in mid-sentence. Her eyes wide open like large dinner plates at the sudden sound from behind her head; along with the feeling of cold metal pressing against the nape of her neck, silenced her.

Jumping up, Rutah retorted, "**DAD! STOP!** This feud you two have must end."

Objecting admittedly, Shane shouted with trauma, "Please, Noah! Stop this nonsense! Killin' Sylvia will complicate the problems and make 'em worse."

Ignoring the objectors, the Game Master plotted his next plan of action. Glaring at his soon to be ex-wife, he challenged her again "Well ... Mastermind; plotter for the control of her husband's material and financial wealth. You'll sign those papers today dear, or you will enjoy being worm food. You see Kelvin here is a skilled sharpshooter. If I give him the signal necessary - you die. It's your choice, pen the papers and live, or party with animals that make soil out of your rotting corpse. Which is it to be? Decide - *NOW!*"

Seconds ticked away in slow rhythmic tempo. *Should I sign or not sign?* This was Sylvia's mental dilemma as she subconsciously bit at her upper lip.

"Still having a problem signing the divorce papers, maybe this might help motivate your hand movements." Pushing a button on a universal remote, the tape deck started to play a tape with two people having a conversation. They were laying down creative plans to ruin the Game Master.

After a minute or two of hearing the tape, GM continued his speech "**You**," emphasizing the point to Sylvia, "**You** had masterminded this scheme almost twenty years ago, dragging Shane into it. Unknown to you both, I was suspicious of your conversations in my absence. Therefore, I placed a concealed tape recorder on the top of the table while I went supposedly to the washroom. It's amazing what modern technology can do these days. What do you think? Such a master minded game of long ago, truly was a grandiose success! **Or,** was that what both of you hoped?"

Sylvia said nothing. She was in disbelief and disturbed that Noah knew about her scheme all these years.

Shane became irritated from being cornered and squirmed in his chair as if in dire need to use the washroom bad.

"Well, what is your decision? Sign …or …**Die**!" GM waited patiently like a cat with all infinity on his side for the juicy mouse.

Rutah now understood her Papa's actions and silently waited for what would next take place.

Realizing she had no choice and lost one possible ace up her sleeve, Sylvia reluctantly signed the papers. When these papers were finally finished with, the empty gun removed to the relief of all concerned.

Two of the attorneys then left with the signed documents in sealed, padded, manila envelopes.

Pushing the remote button again, the tape recorder stopped.

Snarling with volcanic fury, Sylvia steamed because of her lost an ace from her poker hand. *That Bastard's going to pay dearly for that move*, she thought, *still, I have two aces left*.

The coughing began, but subsided after three minutes; allowing time for the Game Master to initiate his next offensive attack.

# CHAPTER 13

# KP - k4 or 75 - 55

Turning slowly, Noah addressed Shane in calm, calculating temperament. "Shane! You and I have a contract to settle. Nineteen years ago, in a restaurant called Sing Soot's Oriental Cuisine, you signed a contract, which was to end within a year's time. Do you remember it?"

Nervous, squirming worse than before and sweating, Shane thought hard. Finally, shaking his head, he spoke, "Uh … No! No…No, I don't remember … I don't remember signing anything!"

"**Contract!**" demanded the baffled Sylvia. **"What contract?"**

"Why, **this contract!**" GM held up a yellowed and creased sheet of paper. Leaning closer, all tried to see what words were on the paper (*except the attorneys and Kelvin*). "The contract stipulates quite clearly, that you owe me money. The agreement states, that within twenty years or less, you would try to sleep with my future wife, as often as possible without my knowing when or where this took place. It also didn't matter whether it was before or after our marriage. As long as you never caught at any time, you would owe me nothing. If you were ever caught at any time, you would pay me the price of my bride - ***One Dollar***."

Jolted off her guard, Sylvia exploded while staring down Shane, "***YOU - SIGNED - WHAT?***"

Shane sank lower into the chair, "*I ... Um... I err... uh ... I ... Um*". Fumbling over what words to say, he finally protested, "Well, I can't remember. ...It was a long time ago."

Glaring with uncontrolled emotional fury, Sylvia couldn't respond to this new startling revelation. Her emotions prevented her from speaking at that moment.

Rutah, who was silent through this whole episode, asked "Why?"

GM continued, "The answer will soon come, *Puddin'*." Smiling ever so subtly, "Shane wanted your mother for himself. Even for the possibility of marriage. In a drunken stupor, he estimated the price of your mother. In his mind - that's all she's worth."

Jumping up, Shane shouted "**LIAR!** Liar, pants on fire! She's far more valuable to me than you could possible know." '*Oops!*' Realizing to late the confession he blurted out, Shane sat down blushing in embarrassment.

Sylvia bowed her head and shook it from side to side. *This is unbelievable,* she thought silently. Glaring back at Shane, *Shane you drunken jackass – where's your brains?*

Pushing another button on a remote control, Noah continued his speech, "There's more!"

"***More?***" the perplexed Sylvia asked.

A panel slid up revealing a jumbo television screen. The TV turned on. The picture seemed split into four smaller screens. One screen in the upper left and right hand corners revealed Shane and Sylvia having sex in different positions, locations, along with different dates, printed on the screen. Embarrassment raced over the guilty parties' faces. Pushing another button the TV went off.

"As can be seen, I did catch Shane with you. The video reveals various locations and time periods over the years." Cold and calculating, the Game Master addressed Shane, "Yes, Shane, you will pay me the money you owe. But don't think I'm finished - **yet!**"

"*Good Lord*, what else could there be!" demanded confused Sylvia, still hurting from the audio, videotape evidence and the news about the unknown contract.

"The contract also stipulated; whether you got caught or not; that I had to sell the deed of the property for an additional dollar." Staring at Shane, "You were the one who insisted on setting the value for the property; no matter how large or small. When the contract was finished, you signed it. Do you **now** remember?"

"I can't remember, I can't remember!" stated Shane in a low terrorized voice.

"Surely you do remember? Here it is." GM handed the contract to Shane in order to jog his foggy memory.

Shane read over the contract, tore it to shreds and threw it into the fireplace. "*Ha!* Now what have you got to say?" demanded the smug Shane.

"That's OK! That copy you tore up was a copy of the original."

Shane's horrified expression was exactly what the Game Master wanted.

"Besides - destroying what you **assumed** to be the original will not cancel the contract legalities. I have a lot more copies available. Would you like to destroy those as well?" Pulling out more folded papers from his pocket, he handed a copy to Sylvia and one to his daughter. "You owe me two bucks! **So pay up Buddy!**"

Reading the contract, Sylvia closed her eyes and shook her head slowly. *Oh no, I lost my second ace,* she thought**,** *to that thieving toad - Shane! That property was to be mine, not his!* Turning to Shane and crumpling the contract at the same time, "This is what you think of me after all these years." She started grabbing various hard objects and books from around the room to throw them at Shane, "You son of the Bitch! You greedy Bastard! How could you think of getting away with it? That property was to be mine, not yours."

*Excellent, another confession* thought the Game Master.

After some individuals ducked from the aerial onslaught of any object not nailed down, Sylvia continued to aim wildly at Shane. Stopping her from doing more damage, Jay finally caught her by both arms from behind. "**Let me go!** I'm going to kill that little psychopathic pervert! **I demand you let me go!**"

"***Excuse me!***" roared the Game Master. "Like I said before, I'm the one who has the floor. I'll do the talking and not you guys!"

Heavy breathing came from both the prey and the predator.

"Those were not your only escapades, where they Shane?" questioned GM.

Shane, sweating more profusely and shaking with intense fear, made no response.

"Well, consider these . . ." pushing another button, the previous two screen quadrants came on with the lower ones showing Shane with different women and men.

Sylvia slumped from the drastic impact of what she was viewing. Submerging deeper into the sinkhole of her chair, she had no idea at all that Shane was a homosexual or even bisexual.

Shane had no idea he was videoed cheating on Sylvia.

After two minutes, the upper two quadrants changed to show Sylvia cheating on Shane with other men and some women.

"*You cheating Slut!*" shouted Shane.

"*You perverted Homo!*" Sylvia retorted.

In fractions of seconds, Shane and Sylvia sprung out of their chairs towards each other, flinging insults at each other while trying to rip each other apart. It was like watching a fur and claw cat fight. The others leapt into the battle lines a minute later and began pulling the two apart. Scratches and ripped clothing showed that a major spat took place.

*Yes,* thought Noah, *I have you both.*

When everyone calmed down from his and her panting, Shane relented. He fished out two dollars from his pocket, shaking nervously, he handed it to the Game Master.

Confirming the payment and completion of the contract, two more attorneys left the building. Shane then parked himself back into the chair he sat in previously wanting to find a hole to crawl into to hide. *How could this happen? Now that I have found out what kind of Jezebel-like scum, Sylvia is!*

Narrowing her eyes, Sylvia's fury turned towards Shane. *You're going to pay for that! You're going to pay dearly;* she fumed.

With a click, the TV was off.

"Congratulations Shane! You now own a wonderful sixty-acre ranch and my ex-wife to boot. Here's the original deed to the property. How does that make you feel?"

Silence now enveloped the room.

# CHAPTER 14

# KB - qb4 or 16 - 43

The coughing started and progressed rapidly. Turning his head and holding a handkerchief to his mouth, the Game Master continued his hacking cough. Rutah sprang to his side; dropping the copy of the contract, in order to hold GM closely. After a moment, GM removed the handkerchief and smiled weakly at his daughter. There on the corners of his mouth was red liquid. The handkerchief also contained red spots in various places. As his breathing returned, he said quietly "I'll be fine *dear*! I'll be fine."

Rutah was uncertain of the validity of her father's statement. Concern furrowed across her face, "Dad", speaking softly, "maybe you should go to the doctor and deal with..." She didn't complete her sentence because the Game Master shook his head 'no'.

Rutah returned to her seat, baffled by what she had seen. *Was that blood I saw?* Worried and anxious, her silent thoughts were for her father.

Sensing her anxiety for him, Noah walked very slowly over to Rutah and knelt down beside her chair. "*Puddin'*- what I've got to share next maybe very hard for you to hear. I hope your heart is big enough to forgive me."

Rutah asked, "Forgive you for what Dad?"

"You've known now for years that you're not my biological daughter?"

Rutah shook her head in agreement. "But how could such knowledge hurt me?"

The Game Master spoke, "It's not the fact that you're not biologically my daughter - *Puddin'*. It was the fact that your birth was both a complete shock and stimulating experience a father could ever have. On the day of your birth, I made a silent and solemn promise to you, that even though you're not biologically my child, I would treat you as though you were my very own. The energy you shared with me all these years empowered me to carry on to this special point in time. I'm just hoping that what I share next will not make you think any less of me. So please - forgive me!" His consoling eyes yearned for her forgiveness.

A tear streamed down her left cheek and a soft "OK!" came out.

While hugging and patting her gently, a soft "Thank you - *Puddin'*" came back.

Turning to his two opponents, the Game Master rose up to continue his aggressive attacks.

Addressing Sylvia, "You were never truly honest with me over the years. You declared that Rutah was my daughter - **biologically**. Tell me, how could that be <u>possible</u>, since you were already three and half months pregnant, before we got married? **Hmm**! Whose child biologically does she belong too?"

Sitting straight up with no expression what so ever, Sylvia replied, "That's for me to know and **none of your damned business!**" Keeping her thoughts to herself, *Ha, I still have this last ace up my sleeve!*

"Oh - but it is my business. You see, I've had Rutah tested, not long after her birth, in order to see if she was my biological daughter. It turns out that she is **100% NOT** my child. She knows this fact, since I was the one who told her years ago. Therefore, the question remains *who really is her biological father.* Until forty-eight months ago, I was not sure. I guessed as to the possible identity of the devious demon. Then I chanced upon the evidence I needed."

*Oh no,* thought Sylvia, *he couldn't have found out!*

"Yes, I found out the Bastard who impregnated you. He left evidence at the scene of his latest dastardly crime. It turns out to be none other than - **Shane!**" GM's coughing started again.

Shane fell out of his chair from shock. He had no idea he was Rutah's biological father.

*Damn, damn, damn,* was all Sylvia could think of before covering her face with her hands. Trying to conceal her shock of his knowing the truth, *shit my last ace lost.*

"*NO!*" cried out Rutah, "That can't be! Not that worthless ***Jackass!***" Tears flowed down her cheeks in raging Tsunami waves. Running out of the ranch house, she headed for the corral fencing. Rivers of tears now flowed blurring her vision making it hard for her to see where she was running too. She slammed into a high wooden fence post.

Noah trailed after Rutah as his coughing slowly subsided. When he reached her, he hugged and consoled Rutah, "I'm sorry - *Puddin'*. It's true! I should've told you earlier. *I'm so sorry*. I know how much you hate the guy, but he's your biological father."

Between sobs, Rutah managed to ask, "Why… couldn't - the test show … it was - you and not - him?"

Holding her closely, he rocked her slowly and saying softly, "I wish it was me. I've loved you all these years as though you were my very own. You're truly special to me - my special empowering *Puddin'*. *I love you so much.* You're highly intelligent and a loving, sensitive young woman. I never ever wanted to hurt you with such news, but I couldn't let you go on living your life without knowing the truth. For the moment, consider," pausing for emphasis and holding her back from his chest, "Shane had physically molested you when you were seven years old, not knowing you were his daughter. You hate him for that and I don't blame you. Yet thanks to Geoffrey and Ben, you regained your joyfulness and at the same time, conquering your nightmares and fears of the dark."

Upon hearing Geoffrey's name, Rutah snapped to attention. Her eyes were gazing into her father's eyes. Suddenly awesome flashbacks of a kind, caring and joyful uncle flooded past her visual cortex. Although Geoffrey was not her biological uncle, he did act like and take on the role of one. He taught her many things over the years about raising and caring for horses. Slowly her tears dissipated and a smile immerged.

Noah seemed to be sensing his daughter's thoughts. He paused to allow her to reflect on her good memories, before he

177

continued speaking. "That's why I stepped in to protect you from his drunken stupidity before he ever harmed you. As for your mother, she was never any help either; she rejected you after the age of two and continues to insult, dominate over and put you down - even today. I filled in the roles of both your *mama* and your *papa*, teaching you all I've learned on how to survive in this strange world. As painful as your life has been, my love for you will not change. I'm hoping it will grow more. They both hate me more than you or themselves!"

"Who could hate a loving person like you - Papa?" sniffled Rutah.

"Those two court jesters in there!" he stated bluntly.

Looking up with wet red eyes, Rutah just smiled back to her father.

"Besides," asked the Game Master, "who's willing to kick the little prick in the pagodas, when I'm gone-eh?"

Both of them started to laugh!

Giving her a final reassuring hug, a light-reassuring kiss, together they turned and walked back to the ranch house. GM's arm was around his daughter's shoulder and her arm around his waist.

## CHAPTER 15

# KRP - kr3 or 78 - 58

Upon re-entering the ranch house, yelling voices pounded the walls. Items of clay, glass or china smashed from flying across the room nearly missing Noah and Rutah. Both parties ducked for cover behind the island counter in the kitchen, avoiding the aerial onslaught.

One Attorney finally caught Sylvia by both arms. She wriggled to escape and do more damage to Shane. The other attorney had to hold back Shane with all his strength. Kelvin, refereeing the battle, finally spoke out in a New York accent, "Silence both of you. You can both kill each other after this is over. **Now sit down and shut up!**"

**"What's going on?"** demanded the Game Master rising up slowly from behind the island counter. Trembling, Rutah took a chance to peer over the island counter top to see if it was safe to stand up or not.

"Just as soon as you left, these two characters tried to remove each other's appendages. I and my legal colleagues had to step in to stop them," replied Jay.

"Well, next time," stated the Game Master sarcastically, "give them both daggers to fight with. It would just speed up the process."

"**Papa!**" replied Rutah with a smirk.

The Game Master smiled back slyly to her, adding a wink.

Kelvin nodded and the attorneys released Sylvia and Shane. Heavy panting coming from the feuding weasels. Bruise marks began to appear, along with flowing blood from several wounds around they faces, arms and legs.

All took their chairs again. This time Sylvia sat at the opposite end of the room from Shane. Shane did the same thing. Their laser beams of hatred, emanating from their eyes, toward each other. While both nursed their various wounds, the static they gave off changed the atmosphere in the room.

"Now, I have one final thing to share… and then I'll leave forever!" GM declared.

As the weasel-like opponents continued to catch their breath, they listened quietly, irritated and fuming.

The Game Master continued, "The ten million dollars that you two hoped to gain access to, according to the audio tape just played earlier, will not happen. You'll never have it!"

"**What?**" Shane cried.

"You've got to be joking! I will have it, **now!** All of it!" demanded Sylvia.

"Why can't they have it, Papa?" Rutah asked.

"Because, *Puddin'*, they already have it in their possession," declared the Game Master.

"How's that possible?" asked the stumped Shane.

"Stop playing your games. Get to the punch line. Cough it up! Where's my money?" demanded the furious Sylvia. "I want it all! I want all ten million dollars' worth, right this moment! Give it to me!"

For the first time, Noah roared with audible laughter. They didn't get the irony of their folly. The roaring from laughter turned eventually to a violent coughing spree, Noah tried to control himself. Rutah noticed more blood on his handkerchief and wanted to come to his aide.

Turning slowly towards his ex-wife, "Come on Mastermind use those lazy grey cells of yours. You've already lost all your aces hidden up your sleeves! Your poker hand is finished. Where do you think the money is located - *huh?* You of all people should already know the answer to your own question."

Looking baffled for a moment, Sylvia could only shrug her shoulders and look away. Since GM knew every move she made, why should she answer him?

"What about you - Shane? You're unable to figure out an answer yet... Let me guess! You're the type of man, who lets his new bride, whom he'd purchased, solve all his financial blunders in life - **Right?**" spoke GM sarcastically. "She'll solve it for you because; to quote her words; '*that dummy has no clue about anything at all - except sex, drugs and alcohol,*' unquote."

Pushing the button to turn on the TV again filled the room with the noises of two people having sex. "Well, what's your answer?"

Shane said nothing and stared at the floor picking at a loose thread in the chair he sat in.

"Here's where it's located," waving his arms around the room. "If you had examined the divorce papers closely, Madame Mastermind, you'd have noticed that the joint bank account was zeroed out, by you, four years ago. There is no money to give! You spent it all on remodelling this building every four years and your expensive life style. **Splurge, splurge,** and **splurge**. That's all you did, spent every last dime, nickel and penny into your selfish dreams." To rub the point in further, GM added, "Which, Shane now personally owns, for a buck!"

Turning to leave with the last attorneys and Jay (*disguised as Kelvin*), the Game Master put in one final plug and deliberately dropped some sheets of paper from the test results, "The test results on Shane, also showed that he is infected with the **AIDS** virus. That's right - good old fashioned - **AIDS!**" rubbing in the point. "His life will be drastically cut short within a year or less," pausing for effect, "and so will yours - *eventually!* Enjoy owning each other, *you love Pigeons!*"

Sinking deeper into her chair, as a defeated opponent, Sylvia began to cry.

Shane let his eyes hit the floor. He couldn't believe there were no monies and now this new shocking turn of events. Sylvia was sure they would get something, but not this kind of offer. He sat there as a lump on a log, ignoring Sylvia's tears of defeat, while listening to their sexual escapades caught on videotape.

As the Game Master reached the door, he turned and looked at Rutah. Her concerned stare looked longingly toward him. Sighing, he signalled for her to come with him. She replied quietly and both left the Nowhere Ranch together.

# CHAPTER 16

# Q - kr5 or 14 - 36

The sun was now setting slowly in the western sky.

"Did the test results indicate anything about me?" inquired Rutah.

Smiling and turning towards her, Noah said, "You're clean! Just like me."

They headed toward the new SUV.

Stopping for a moment, GM's coughing began and intensified. Rutah held on to him to prevent him from falling over.

"*Damn, the doc was wrong about this one,*" he mumbled.

"What was that - Papa?" Rutah inquired.

"Oh nothing!" he waved off. "Dear, would you be so kind as to drive me into town?"

"Sure Dad!" grabbing the keys she ran to start the new SUV. The coughing continued and his face began to pale ever so slightly.

Gasping with each breath, Noah slowly slid into the passenger side. As Rutah ran around to slip into the driver's side, GM signalled the others to meet at the appointed stop.

Grabbing another clean handkerchief, turning his head away, his coughing persisted in annoying stops and starts. Wiping his face, this handkerchief was also turning red like the last one.

Rutah started the SUV and they headed down the gravel road towards town.

"What did you mean when you said the doctor was wrong?" inquired Rutah again.

Looking at her puzzled and concerned face, the Game Master calmly stated, "I could never hide anything from you. I meant that his timing is off," coughing again. "My time left is much shorter than was originally calculated."

Bowled over by his answer, Rutah sought more details. "What are you trying to say **Papa**? Your time here on Earth is going to end?"

"Yes, that's exactly what I mean," coughing between breaths. His face was taking on an even paler colour than before.

"Hold on, I'll get you to the doctor" retorted Rutah.

"*No*" came a weak reply, "stop at our favourite parking spot, on Seven Mile Hill."

Rutah threw a bewildered and puzzled look his way.

"*Please - Puddin'*" he pleaded.

"All right, but I don't see how it's going to help you."

Driving around several twists and turns, she finally came to a stop, on a hill, overlooking the Sunshine Valley. The Valley's beauty seemed to stretch for miles, except for the patches of forest obscuring some viewpoints around the parking lot. Beside the large open gravel-parking area, and near the trail was a pile of chopped wood, a wheelbarrow and

Jay's vehicle. She ran to the other side to help her dad out of the SUV.

"I just want to show you something, down the trail, in our favourite meadow."

Walking quietly beside and holding him up, Rutah never said a word. After following the trail for ten minutes, they came to a large meadow clearing. In the centre was an orderly pile of wood with a plank of lumber on top. Surrounding its base was a trench, filled with water and rocks around the outside of the trench, to prevent the spread of the fire to come.

"*There*" he pointed weakly.

Wondering about the pile, she said nothing and led him to it. Without realizing it, she never noticed the other three people from the house were there as well.

The coughing never stopped during the whole time. It came on stronger and GM's voice seamed to get weaker.

Crawling on top of the wood, he exclaimed between coughing and spitting up red fluid, "This is my funeral pyre. I want my human remains to be cremated here," pointing to the surroundings, "where we had so many fond memories."

Tears started to fill her eyes. "*There. There Puddin'! Don't cry!* My time is almost over. I've had to speed up the divorce and contract proceedings because I knew my time's slipping away. *Unfortunately, it's coming faster than I thought.*"

Tears now flowed from her eyes, "**No, not now!**"

The fluid buildup started to make it harder for him to speak much longer, "*Kelvin will tell you what my second last request will be....*"

Collapsing onto his back, the Game Master slowly and painfully expired.

Falling to her knees Rutah cried out, "No, no, no!" The torrential downpour roared from her eyes. "**No, no, no**" was all she could say while beating the pyre.

Jay bent over and consoled her. When she finally regained her composure, she rose from the ground, and then she proceeded to cross her father's arms over and kissed him tenderly and lovingly on the forehead.

Wiping slow trickling tears from her eyes, she turned to Jay and asked, "What was my Papa's second to last request?"

Jay held her arm and slowly walked her back to the SUV. "Your father told me to tell you, that the new SUV you just drove - is yours. He bought, paid for it fully and put it into your name yesterday. The next thing he instructed me to tell you was to collect the wood piled up by the wheelbarrow and cover his remains with the wood. Inside the SUV, there a small red can of gasoline. He wanted you to soak the funeral pyre the best way you could and ignite it. That was his second to last wish."

Just shaking her head up and down in agreement, she followed beside Jay to the pile of wood. Tears still flowed slowly down her cheeks on their way back.

The various oranges and crimson reds filled the evening sky.

Twenty-seven minutes later, Jay (*disguised as Kelvin*) and Rutah returned with the remaining wood and small Jerry can. The snail-paced shadows cast such awkward dances across the body that almost no one seemed to notice a flower inserted into GM's left vest pocket.

Within seven more minutes, the funeral pyre was alight. Its intense flames cast both powerful light and intense heat in all directions. The smoke that also ascended billowed into the evening darkness.

"Good bye – Papa," tears falling like rain down her cheeks once more, as she backed away from the intense heat.

As Rutah cried, the female attorney came over to hold her.

An hour had slipped by. The flames began to descend lower than before as ashes began to pile up.

Slowly, one person at a time, before leaving the scene, gave their condolences to Rutah. Jay stayed an extra twenty-two minutes before he spoke to her.

"Your dad wanted me to give you this." He handed a small key to a locker. "He told me to tell you, that he left you something of importance at the train station." Turning, Jay left.

Rutah was finally all alone with her thoughts. *This was too sudden. This was all too sudden!*

She stayed until there were only burning embers left. She turned and headed toward the SUV, as the full moon rose above the horizon, beyond the Sunshine Valley.

# CHAPTER 17

# QRP - qr4?? or 71 - 51??

Rutah arrived at the **Slim Star Train Station** around 9:42 PM. The key's number was for locker number twenty-eight. For a modern station, the place seemed deserted except for the station attendants, the cleaning personal and an old woman knitting something in a comfortable waiting room chair.

Standing at the canteen was a scruffy old prospector buying a coffee. Rutah could tell he was a prospector, by the metal gold pan attached to his old canvas backpack and the pickaxe sticking out the top of the pack. *It's amazing the different kinds of people a person can come across*, she thought to herself.

Rutah took in a deep breath and then proceeded to search for locker number twenty-eight. Within two minutes, she found it. Inserting the key, she turned it and found some papers in a manila envelope and a large gym bag.

Looking around to see if anyone was watching; no one was; she slipped the envelope into her purse to read later. She reached in to pull out the gym bag only to have the heavy thing almost slam her onto the floor. Rutah felt some of the wind knocked out of her lungs.

She stood up and tried to pick up the bag. Unsuccessful! *Now what am I going to do? This damn thing is heavy!* She tried a couple of more times, without success, except for breathing heavier and sweating profusely.

A strange deep gravely, twang type voice spoke beside her, "Are yah ok - *Mis*? Would yah like some halp, dear?"

Turning rapidly from being startled, Rutah came face to face with the old prospector man, whose back was to her earlier. His rugged and pruned face showed his age, along with the dark skin indicating his continual baking in the sun. Semi-white hair, two chipped front teeth and one patch on his left eye met her gaze.

Paralysed for the briefest of moments, Rutah was not sure what to say, except very hesitantly, "Thank you - kind sir. I would … I would be honoured for your assistance."

Bending over to pick up the bag, a grunting sound parted from the old man's lips. Yet with graceful ease, he picked up the gym bag as though he lifted heavy weights or boulders before.

"Where'd yah like it taken to - Mis?" queried the kind old man.

"You could take it to my vehicle just outside" she replied.

"Very good - Mis. Pleez lead the way!"

She opened the side door of the SUV and the old prospector toss in the heavy bag onto the floor. She closed the door and thanked the old man again. He bowed ever so slightly to her.

Then, a few tears trickled down her cheeks again. *Damn it, I wish I could stop crying and control myself better - especially in front of this kind stranger.*

The old man saw her tears, "Pardon me - Mis. May an old prospector ask if yare ok? Yah seem distraught about sumethin'. I 'm old, yet strong as a mule. Mees hearin' is still acute and I'm a patient lizzener to those who wish to spake."

"I don't want to trouble you with my problems."

"Trouble! **Trouble?** Mis, yare no trouble at all to the likes me, old James Rabbit. My friends call me 'Dodger' cause I like to move quickly over the prospectin' fields. Dodge over here or dodge over there! Besides, I have three hours before me train arrives. Pleez, allow me to treat yah to a coffee in the canteen and tell old Jim your problem."

Rutah was hesitant at first. Her father taught her to be careful about strangers, but old Dodger didn't strike her as a mean or dangerous man. *His manners though, were definitely from some ancient school of antique thought and manners*, she figured. Yet a person seemed to feel more pity for him than running away from him.

She accepted the invitation, "Yes. I'd be delighted too", she paused, "…Dodger!"

Smiling, Dodger looped his arm so she could slide hers through. Wiping tears away, she accepted his dusty ragged and patched coated arm. *Yes, most definitely from the ancient school of manners. His mannerism indicates a man who does not act like a rapist or assassin!*

Quietly, they entered the station together, arm in arm.

# CHAPTER 18

# Qxkb7# or 36x76#

Finding a table with a view, Dodger purchased an extra coffee, sandwiches and some treats. Sitting together, Dodger asked, "I don't mean to pry into yare personal businezz - Mis. However, old Dodger does get bothered when he seez youthful lassies, such as yarself, distressed over sumethin'. How may I halp yah find yare joy again?"

*Strange!* She thought, *He's so concerned about my depressed state, yet he never asked what caused it. He seems almost like someone I know....*

She took a deep breath and a chance by opening up to Dodger, "Well - It began like this...."

Time slid by and the two were so engrossed in Rutah's story, they failed to notice the steady increase in people hoping to catch the Midnight Express Line.

Finally she ended with "... so, here I am."

Sitting back quietly, Dodger finally spoke slowly as if to no one in particular, "I'd say that yare foster dad truly luved yah and hoped to give yah the best of wat he could - knowledge, edumacation, possibly financial halp, his pride for yah and . . ."

pausing for effect, "his last dyin' wish - unconditional luv." Looking straight at Rutah, "I think he wanted yah to succeed in yare life and he probably had planned sumethin' wunderful fur yah. He may have wanted yah to have a head start. Besides, I should know, I've got children meself." Dodger seemed to be looking off into space now, reminiscing, "Yes, all of 'em have, to a certain degree, become successful. I'm proud of 'em. It never mattered to me nun if they became rich or poor. I luv 'em all and continue to hope nuthin' but good and peace come to 'em …." his voice trailed off.

"That's so sweet! Are you going to visit them soon?" she questioned.

As if snapped out of a daze, Dodger came back to reality. "I … I'm sorry Mis. Did yah ask me a question?"

Smiling she asked, "Yes! Are you going to visit them?"

"Yes, I am *Niddup*. Yes, I am!"

Dodger said that word so fast, Rutah wasn't sure she heard him clearly. She was about to ask him what word he called her, when the announcement came over the loud speaker; '*The Midnight Express is now ready for boarding. Please have your tickets ready. The Midnight Express is now ready for boarding.*'

"That's me call!" stated Dodger as he stood up. "I hope to meet yah again *Mis…?*" he asked, as his voice trailed off.

"Rutah … my name is Rutah Body."

"It's been a pleasure!" Dodger replied, taking her hands and kissing them. He next picked up his canvas backpack, he heading for the train. Looking back quickly and waving, Dodger stated, "I hope yare father gave yah sumethin' wunderful to remember him by. See yah around, *Niddup!*"

Dodger disappeared into the mingling crowd.

Puzzlement crossed over Rutah's forehead. *Niddup? What did Dodger mean by that strange word?* Shaking her head in bewilderment, she rose up slowly and headed back to her SUV.

= = =

Dodger never went aboard the train; instead, he turned the corner and headed for a GMC Truck parked in the parking lot. Throwing his old canvas backpack into the passenger's seat, Dodger climbed into the driver's seat. From this vantage point, he could watch Rutah as she drove off in her SUV.

"Good-bye - *Puddin'!*" exclaimed a youthful voice.

Removing the eye patch over his left eye, the false teeth and peeling off the false face, Dodger was no longer Dodger. That old prospector's gravelly voice vanished also.

"**Check Mate. I Win!**" declared the Game Master with profound glee.

As if by magic, the front windshield spelt out digital numbers totalling seven and a half million dollars. Then the sound of a *Cha-Ching* occurred. A number two appeared before the first number seven and an additional two dollars simultaneously appeared at the end of his total worth.

The Game Master roared with laughter and drove off in the opposite direction from Rutah. His destination - anywhere the wind blew northward.

## CHAPTER 19

# Freedom at Last!

Sylvia sat close to the fireplace, sipping her favourite poison, to drown her sorrows and failures. Beside her was a coffee table stacked with a small set of old high school yearbooks. Grabbing the first one on top of the pile, she opened it from the back pages, reminiscing about her past senior years, while slowly progressing to the front of the book. Finding her photo, there was a dedication written to her below the photo. It stated things such as *...your bank accounts ... emptied - people*, and *...great at masterminding challenging school events.* "Yeah - right," she mumbled to herself.

The next photo she came upon was Shane's ugly zit filled mug. His little caption stated *...not to be trusted*, and *Watch out girls, Shane's on the prowl.* "Definitely his *modus operandi*," she mumbled.

Shane had retreated to the kitchen table, beside the adjoining living room, with the health report before him. Under the medium setting of the kitchen light, he looked deeply forlorn and remained silent. For the first time, he was sober, staring at a glass of water and pondering what to do next.

No longer able to cope, but to face the fact, they had both lost big time. As for his voracious sex drive, it stamped its brakes to a squealed halt, unable to advance forward.

Rutah drove back home. Very exhausted and distressed, she quietly entered the ranch house. No one had noticed her arrival. The TV was off and a powerful silent shadow covered the entire building. Occasionally a low mumble or cry would shatter this darkened setting.

Sylvia finally turned to a page with GM's youthful picture and underneath was a caption dedicated to him, from his closest friends. It read in part *...to the best Game Master of Chess, Pool, Poker and Puzzles. By outwitting and outplaying others, may success continue in your direction - always!* Her blood pressure rose and her face turned red, "That **moron**...was a **Game Master**? How dare he beat me ..." Insanity seemed to settle in, like an unwanted companion. No wonder she lost! A brilliant Game Master, who outwitted and outplayed her successfully, defeated Sylvia. In a final fit of rage and defiance, she flung the yearbook into the fireplace. "So - There!" she stated to herself, as if talking to no one in particular. She then got up to refill her glass with more intoxicating fluid.

Rutah now spoke to both of them. She informed them of his death and cremation; precisely as GM had calculated she would do. Rutah also told them that she was packing and leaving for good.

Pouring more Whiskey into her glass, Sylvia only grunted in her drunken state and half-heartedly waved a *bon voyage*. She turned, staggered and parked herself back down into her chair. She was too drunk to care anymore. She just watched the final ashes falling from the burning yearbook, and produced occasional low mournful groans of defeat.

Shane tried reasoning with Rutah to stay.

"Not after what evil things you did to me!" fumed Rutah. "I'm not staying with sick, demented failures of life - *like you two*. You're neither my true father", she said to Shane, "nor are you my true mother", she stated to Sylvia. "Don't try to stop me! My real father died tonight at your expense. It cost me his love and devotion, while it cost him his life. You're both twisted and perverted individuals; yes, you need each other - ***BADLY!***"

Sylvia then grabbed the next book in the stack, skimming slowly through it, still drinking her poison, reminiscing about the past and mumbling again. When she finished that book, it too would enjoy a fiery grave, along with all the others - one at a time, ignoring Rutah's statements.

Shane didn't react either. He let his eyes drop to the floor and parked his butt onto the stool he was previously sitting on.

Since they never showed any consideration or compassion for the loss of the father she loved, Rutah stormed over to her old room, locked the door and started packing the belongings she wanted to take with her. Within twenty minutes, she left her room for the last time and headed for the front door. Just before exiting, Rutah glanced back with these dagger-like words, "*I hate you both!* Don't either of you ever try to seek me out." Shoving her point even deeper, "You'll never find me and I'll never allow either of you back into my life - **Ever!**"

Slamming the door, she headed over to the staff quarters for more of her belongings. When she was finished there, she jumped into her SUV and was gone - forever.

CHAPTER 20

# Activating those
# Grey Cells

Five hours later, cutting across Washington State, Rutah reached the intersection of Interstate Highway #101. She pulled over into the nearest campground off the highway. Stretching out and finding the most comfortable position possible, she cried herself to sleep. Exhaustion had over taken her within six minutes.

Seven more hours passed, when Rutah awoke. Stretching her stiff muscles and joints, she headed south on Highway #101 to find a trucks stop or a restaurant to eat in. She didn't care what she ate, just as long as it silenced her turbulent, grumbling stomach.

She finally pulled into *Jack's Cuisine & Truck Stop*. *Food at last,* she thought.

After eating her fill, Rutah ordered a jumbo coffee to go and then headed back to the SUV. Before leaving the parking lot, she decided to examine the contents in the manila envelope.

Inside was a *Last Will and Testament*, copies of four health reports, along with detailed genetic test results of the Game Master, Shane and herself. There were also various photos and a small yellow piece of notepaper.

Being the systematic daughter, she began with the will. She found it had the usual standard wording, but the final page ripped in half, width wise.

*Strange, why do that?*

As for the four health reports, Shane and Sylvia were definitely sick people - AIDS mainly. Rutah was clean. GM was overall ok, but the doctor diagnosed him with Tuberculosis.

*That's what killed Papa!*

The genetic tests showed that Shane was her biological father and not GM. This news made her heart yearn even more for the deceased Game Master.

Several photos were of the Game Master and herself over the years. Some of their wild adventures were on horseback, bicycles, hiking and swimming. Others were of locations they'd visited, over school lessons he taught her.

*Yes, Papa loved to teach me all he knew,* she reminisced.

Then she turned her attention to the strange yellow notepaper. The entire note said, *"Didn't you look in the gym bag yet?"*

*The Gym bag,* she almost forgot about it.

Reaching over the seat to where it lay on the floor, she opened it to reveal a large quantity of wrapped money, a digital video Camcorder and the torn half of paper with words printed on it. Rutah struck dumb and speechless, knew not what to say. *There's no way! This can't be happening to me*, she thought. *How much is in there?*

Picking up the paper, it read, "All 2 ½ Million Dollars are for you and you alone. I don't want your mother or Shane getting their greedy paws on it. I managed to salvage this amount for you before your mother spent it all. Use it wisely. Spend it frugally. This is your new beginning - my *Puddin'*. I love you!" It was signed Apap!

Setting the paper on the passenger seat, she thought, *Apap. What does apap mean?*

Grabbing the Camcorder, Rutah zipped up the gym bag and sat back down in the front seat. Hitting the play button, GM's face appeared. He spoke to her as though he was right beside her. His gentle voice always calmed her. He gave a lengthy speech, interjecting with odd finger gestures now and then. He ended it with, ". . . I hope you use this money to start your new adventures without me. I'm confident you'll succeed - *Niddup*. Remember - don't forget the number one. I love you - *Niddup!*"

The video stopped there.

*Niddup! Niddup? That had a familiar ring to it.* Thinking hard, it finally hit her. *Wait a minute; was that not the same name the Old Dodger used?*

Looking up, Rutah saw another vehicle wanting to take her parking space. Signalling her intention by waving and backing out, she surrendered her parking stall.

Turning left and heading south down Highway #101, Rutah tried to figure out these bizarre words. *What is apap and niddup?*

Once her Styrofoam mug was empty and she searched for a garbage receptacle to toss it out. She noticed a sign indicating a rest stop, one mile ahead. Pulling in and a little further past the garbage receptacle, she jumped out to ditch the mug.

When Rutah re-entered her SUV, her eyes happened to look into the rear-view mirror, showing a sight she didn't expect. The words on the garbage receptacle were backwards.

A flash of lightning struck her in the brain with a major jolt.

*That's it! The words are backwards.*

Grabbing a piece of paper and a pencil, she rewrote *apap* as "papa" and *niddup* as "Puddin".

*That's what your scheme is! You're playing a mirror image puzzle game with me.* Rutah smirked to herself, *Papa; you always loved playing your games.*

Another thought struck her. She reviewed the video a second time. At one point in the video, Rutah noticed a flower, three times in a row, appearing and disappearing from his left vest pocket. Also near the end of the video, the word *"niddup"* appears on the screen for four seconds and then it vanished.

Rutah rewound the video to count the weird finger gestures for the third time. Writing it down, it seemed to make up a phone number, the only thing missing was the number one in front of it.

*I'll call that number later.*

A smile gradually crossed her face. She finally remembered the flower she noticed in the vest pocket. When he died in front of her, there was no flower in the pocket. Upon returning to the body, her mind noted, but blocked out the flower that magically appeared there.

*Papa, you aren't dead after all. You're alive! You never had Tuberculosis! Yet, how was this possible, since I saw you expire?*

Still searching for an answer, Rutah reminded herself that this was only a game. *You wanted me to figure out the clues to your puzzle. The answer is to call the number you gave me!*

Shaking her head in amazement and smiling, Rutah started the SUV and pulled out of the rest stop. Driving in the same southerly direction as before, she was excited.

*Today, I begin my new life!*

# EPILOGUE

Both Shane and Sylvia finally departed their ways.

They unanimously decided to split the sale of the property between themselves, almost totalling One Million Dollars. Taking his half, Shane knew his time was short. Therefore, he went on to spend half of it foolishly, while the rest went to wine, women and song (*not to mention drugs*). There were times he just gave money away, to either local charities or the local winos, sums totalling as much as, three thousand dollars at a time or more.

Seven months later, the local **Custard Tribune** had an article write up about a local man, in his late thirties or early forties found dead in a back alley. The paper claimed that Shane had died of both overdosing on drugs and exposure to the elements, since this was late November. A third of a bottle of Vodka was in his right hand, and a needle was still stuck in his left arm. His wallet contained only two dollars; similar to the last two dollars he invested in Sylvia and the property.

What an investment!

As for Sylvia, she slowly went mad. The disease began to take its toll on her mentally and physically. She moved to Montana in order to get the medical help she needed. After two years, most of her money spent on hospital bills, although she did save a small amount for any funeral expenses. Otherwise, she had left nothing behind.

Sylvia's anger was towards herself mostly, for allowing a bitter defeat she experienced by the Game Master. He did refer to her as a 'mastermind' of various strategies and games. She too, believed she was one, until this ultimate defeat. Now all she could do was wither away in frustration, anger and hopelessness for being an utter failure at not winning with her poker hand.

While on her deathbed and during her delirious moments, Sylvia did call out for Rutah from time to time. She seemed to be pleading for her daughter's forgiveness. Unfortunately, Rutah never heard such pleas.

= = =

The scenery was phenomenal on Rutah's long drive to Northern California. Adding to its beauty, the refreshing odours of the salty Pacific Ocean air combining with the odours of the Cedar Wood Rain Forests, along the coasts of Washington and Oregon States, stimulated her senses.

Freedom, along with a new outlook, awakened her love of life.

Only one thing still disquieted her thoughts as she drove onward.

*How the hell, did you do it – Papa?*[7]

## To Be Continued!

---

[7]     This is the last challenge in this novel. Go to Appendix "G" for encouragement.

# APPENDIX "A"

According to the **14<sup>th</sup> Edition** of the **Brewer's Dictionary of Phrase & Fable**, © 1989 - The word *Nobby* means: **smart, elegant, neat**: taken from *NOB*, a slang term for one of the upper classes, a contraction of *noble* or *nobility*.

# APPENDIX "B"

Well, have you figured out the answers yet? This is your challenge! Try to use your grey cells to figure out the answers.

Below are the same two mathematical questions, which Noah presented as a challenge to his opponents. Also included is an additional question for the fun of it. See if you can solve them.

1. How do you get four 6's to total the sum of 30?
$$6, 6, 6 \ \& \ 6 = 30$$

2. How do you get five 5's to total the sum of 6?"
$$5, 5, 5, 5 \ \& \ 5 = 6$$

3. How do you get seven 7's to total the sum of 100?
$$7, 7, 7, 7, 7, 7 \ \& \ 7 = 100$$

4. How do you get five 8's to total the sum of 2?
$$8, 8, 8, 8 \ \& \ 8 = 2$$

5. How do you get five numbers to total the sum of 22?
$$9, 6, 3, 5, 8 = 22$$

Still stuck! Well here is a hint:

Start with the first number from the list above. When you use it up, cross it off the list before using the next number beside it. Continue with the remaining numbers from the list.

Cross each one off as you use them up until no numbers are left and you have worked out the answer asked for.

Keep working on them. I'm confident you can find the answer to the questions.

Do you still need a clue - Eh?

Turn to the next page!

**Sorry!**

You will have to wait until Novel #3 for
the answers to all three questions.

# APPENDIX "C"

How about the question Shawn gave to Noah? Here is part of the problem again!

> *... ten customers came rushing in at 10:55 am. They needed a loaf of bread immediately. Mr. Bordeaux was more than willing to accommodate these customers; the only problem was he had just nine loaves left instead of ten. Since he ran out of flour earlier that day, he would be unable to make any more loaves until possibly after the war (or if his bakeshop was still standing).*
>
> *The customers bickered over who should get a loaf and who should not. Tempers flew and the baker had a major challenge to calm everyone down. The high stress levels were rampant in the air due to the threat of the German invasion soon to arrive. Ordering everyone present to be silent, the baker carried the nine loaves to his kitchen counter. Laying the loaves out in three rows of three loaves, he puzzled over this dilemma. After five minutes, Mr. Bordeaux*

*finally came up with a possible solution to the problem.*

*[At this point in the story, the average person would consider that cutting off one-tenth of each loaf would achieve the desired effect. If a person did not mind eating all heals (or crusts) then this would have accommodated the request. However, to make the divisions fare, no one individual could receive all heals (or crusts) of the bread.]*

*Therefore, Mr. Bordeaux devised a way to portion out and wrapped up each loaf in such a manner that each customer received a loaf of bread. Leaving satisfied the customers paid for their loaf and left the bakery. As for the baker, Mr. Bordeaux turned over the closed sign on his shop door, locking the doors, pulled down the blinds by 11:59 am.*

*How did this French Baker accommodate his final customers in distributing the nine loaves evenly amongst ten workingmen? What are the correct portions of bread Mr. Bordeaux came up with so each worker received his individual loaf?*

***Hint**: Remember, each person has to receive at least two heals of bread.*

Try to work this one out carefully.

Noah came up with the answer rapidly because Shawn didn't realize that GM had already taken the same book out of the school library seven weeks earlier.

Can you figure out this tough one? Come on! Try this challenge! I'm sure you can do it!

Are you still in search of a clue to this question?

Turn to the next page!

**Sorry!**

You'll have to wait for the third novel to get
the answer for this complex exam.

# APPENDIX "D"

While lying in a hospital bed with a broken leg, stock market annalist Ralph Nelson Elliott was bored with his predicament. Requesting the stock market section of the newspaper, Mr. Elliott began to study a few stocks to see if there was something to markets ups and downs or not. After a few weeks of observation and analysis, he discovered a repetitive cycle to the trades of stocks that later developed into the Elliott Wave Theory.

One has to remember that during the 1920's; most people believed that the stock market behaved in a somewhat chaotic manner. Mr. Elliott's Wave Theory proved otherwise.

The Wave Theory works when stocks go up or down during these repetitive cycles. He also noted that the emotions of investors: as a cause of outside influences or a predominant psychology of the masses of the time: affected these same cycles. Elliott claimed that the upward and downward swinging of the mass psychology always followed these same repetitive patterns, which he graphed out as waves.

The Wave's general cycle starts at position #1 (*lower left*) and moves upward in a seesaw pattern to the #5 position known as *five up*. Then a correction pattern takes over and a ***three down*** pattern takes place (*from position A, moving* *down to position C*). Then the cycle repeats over again at the #1 position as a 5-3 (*or 5 up & 3 down*) move. This is what and how the Elliott Wave Theory pattern generally looks like and functions. From its adaptable form, most investors can predict the approximate occasion to either buy stocks (*during an up wave: positions 1, 3, 5 &B*) or sell stocks (*as the wave goes down: positions 2, 4, A & C*).

If you want more details about this subject, please consult your local library or the Internet for more information about the *Elliott Wave Theory* or *Ralph Nelson Elliott*.

# APPENDIX "E"

To challenge the women to these questions, Noah wanted to see who would win the quest of knowledge he had laid out. Since Sylvia was going to be the only one to succeed according to GM's plans, Noah didn't reveal the answer to this riddle.

See if you can solve it!

**I once saw the sun, but never twice in lore.**
**I was soft, then hard, then soft once more.**
**What event describes me and evens a score?**

Can you guess what the answer might be? It requires a lot of thinking to solve it.

Ok, ok! For those of you racking your brains over it, I will give you this clue: if you have not already guessed by now, this comes from a library of 66 books - compiled into one volume – which some families own a copy of, but it just collects dust sitting on the shelf.

The answer you seek will come at another time. Check out one of the later novels for the answer. Now, just try, if you can, to solve it in the meantime.

Have fun figuring it out!

# APPENDIX "F"

If you haven't figured out from which game these moves are from, I'll tell you.

It is a war game called Chess! A board game played between to players (*or opponents*). One player uses light chess figurines, while the other opponent uses dark ones. If a person wants to know how to play this game in more detail, check any Chess Book in your local library or the Internet on the rules to this game. Some of the expressions (*codes*) used during play are below:

<u>*Key for Chess Moves*</u>:

| | |
|---|---|
| K = King | k = king's… |
| Q = Queen | q = queen's… |
| B = Bishop | b = bishop's… |
| N = Knight | n = knight's… |
| R = Rook (*Castle*) | r = rook's… |
| P = Pawn | 'x' = Take or Capture |
| '+' = Check | '#' = Checkmate |
| '!' = Good move | '?' = Bad move |
| '??' = Blunder move | '0-0' = K-side castle |
| '0-0-0' = Q-side castle | |

## A Simplified Board Set Up:

### White Side

| | | | | | | | |
|---|---|---|---|---|---|---|---|
| **11** | *12* | **13** | *14* | **15** | *16* | **17** | *18* |
| *21* | **22** | *23* | **24** | *25* | **26** | *27* | **28** |
| **31** | *32* | **33** | *34* | **35** | *36* | **37** | *38* |
| *41* | **42** | *43* | **44** | *45* | **46** | *47* | **48** |
| **51** | *52* | **53** | *54* | **55** | *56* | **57** | *58* |
| *61* | **62** | *63* | **64** | *65* | **66** | *67* | **68** |
| **71** | *72* | **73** | *74* | **75** | *76* | **77** | *78* |
| *81* | **82** | *83* | **84** | *85* | **86** | *87* | **88** |

### Black Side

## Simplified Chess Board Positions:

**15** or 85 = King(s) positions

14 or **84** = Queen(s) positions

**13**, 16, 83 and **86** = Bishops positions

12, **17, 82** and 87 = Knights positions

**11**, 18, 81 and **88** = Rooks positions

21 - **28** and **71** - 78 = Pawns positions

Therefore using the Key for Chess Moves, a move like KP-k4 would mean **King's Pawn** (*pawn in front of King*) moves to **King's 4** (*or the pawn moves 2 squares forward from its previous position in front of the King to a square that is the fourth position in front of the King*).

The same move is 25 - 45 (*check the chart on previous page*). Try this game sometime!

It has quite a history behind it and the various strategies for winning against or tying your opponent.

Please Note: The person with the white (*or light coloured*) chess pieces always make the first move.

# APPENDIX "G"

If you were in Noah's shoes, how would you have engineered this feat?

While answering Rutah's question, can you uncover the clues or even try to guess at any possibilities of how this mystery could have taken place?

Given time and meditation on the subject, I am sure the solution will become clear to you! Otherwise, you will have to wait for the answer in the third novel of this trilogy!

# EXCERPT FROM BOOK 2 – THE CRYPTIC WILL

## Hawk's Tribute

It was the summer of 1987. The sweltering heat of that July week was unbearable. Not one rain cloud formed in the sky to cool down the valley cauldron. If a person didn't have their Air Conditioning units turned on, they felt like they would die of heat stroke or melt into the softened street pavement.

Despite the heat wave, Canoe Corner was a buzzing hive of activity especially around the courthouse. Dubbed by the local newspapers of the time as the crime of the decade; since few crimes took place in Canoe Corner or Artichoke; this event stood out in the two townships.

The trial was presided over by the middle aged and newly appointed judge to the territory *Judge Karl Nippon*. Mister Nippon had moved into Artichoke eight months prior and he was hoping to avoid being involved in anything more than traffic violations or minor incidences in the valley. He was wrong! When this murder came forward, the two towns in question went into action to duke it out in court.

As the local District Attorney, **Rylan Nodal** was determined to prove his case in court. He believed without any inkling of doubt that Salishan **Hawk Feather Rosebush** was guilty of murdering a Blackfoot co-worker **Roger High Hill**, the attempted murder of his boss and billionaire landowner **Kendrick A. Curtains**. Although his evidence in the case was flimsy at best, Rylan was determined to make every effort to impress his peers.

Attorney for the defendant; **Michelle Upright** was even more determined to prove Hawk Feather's innocence and that the charges against her client should be dropped, so that the real culprit can be found and brought to justice.

Sitting behind the defendant's box was Fawn Rosebush, the sister to Hawk Feather and who was eleven years old at the time. Their only other living relative at that time was their grandfather **Buckaroo "Big Buck" Dancer**.

The Sheriff at the time was a man named **Justin A. Corridor**. He was a gorilla shaped man with bulging muscles and a bad attitude. His fiery temper showed how much he hated anyone who was not Caucasian. His greying hair and piercing blue eyes; just like the natural blue eyes of British actor **Ed Bishop**; could slice a person into pieces before he spoke a word. He hated criminals and any form of injustice to the district he lived in. His gruff manner well known to the locals in both communities and most people avoided crossing his path at any time. Their usual saying about this man was if *you see the sheriff coming – split the scene fast and don't look back.*

For the past week, both attorneys fought a long and hard battle to prove their sides of the case. Just like the card game

Euchre, both attorneys jostled for a trump hand; let alone power playing with the trump card in order to win their hand.

As the battle progressed, the District Attorney seemed to gain great grounds in the first two days of the trial. Nodal's persuasive personality goaded the jurors to take his side right from the beginning of the trial. Yet as time went on, he began losing his footing from the mounting contradictory evidence. Knowing he had a losing hand, Rylan continued to fight to the bitter end, leaving him only one way out - a mistrial.

Michelle held herself back from aggressively attacking Rylan's claims on her client. Like a feline ready to pounce on the mouse at the appropriate time, she used her feminine charms to gain the upper hand. Although subtle in her methods, this black haired woman was not going to give up that easily. To beat her opponent's hand, she needed the trump card and an ace to win. Both of these cards, she held and was ready to use at the appropriate moment. When the time arrived, Michelle pulled off her victory with the testimony of Kendrick A. Curtains and the ballistics report.

When the billionaire took the stand, Mister Curtains claimed he was helping Hawk Feather replace five old fence posts on the southeast corner of his property, at the time of Hill's murder. Not only did it take half of the day to do the job, but also both men had to add additional reinforcement materials to the fence posts so they would not rot away as quickly as they did in the marshy soil of that area of his property. As for Mister Curtains wounds, later that evening, he knew that Hawk Feather was at a dance with all the other cowhands. The dance held on his ranch that evening as a way to congratulate the workers for their hard efforts to keep the ranch going for the past year.

When Michelle used the ballistic information, the bullet that hit Mister Curtains' right shoulder didn't match the one found in Hill's body. The bullet that hit Mister Curtains was a 22-calibre slug, shot at close range, while Mister Hill's body was full of 12-gage buckshot.

As the ballistics report indicated, Sheriff Corridor left the courtroom quietly and fumed all the way to his office. He didn't wait for the verdict to be read; he already knew what the outcome would be. The investigation into the murder of Mr. Hill and attempted murder of Mr. Curtains would have to go on, until the real culprit located.

When the twelve-person jury read the verdict, Hawk Feather Rosebush pronounced innocent of all charges and released back into the community. The people of Artichoke were ecstatic with joy since one of their own found not guilty.

As for the people in Canoe Corner, they scowled at the verdict. They wanted to have an old-fashioned hanging in town and it wasn't going to happen.

= = = =

The people in Artichoke gave a small parade through town the next day, throwing confetti, setting off fireworks and releasing helium balloons for the newly freed man; Mister Rosebush. This was not just a party about freedom for Hawk, a tribute to the justice system and the times when it proves the innocence of a person.

Mister Curtains paid for the whole affair and everyone in Artichoke invited to attend this special day.

Later that evening, a huge banquet was set up in the park in Hawk's honour.

Unknown to the cheering crowd, a lone rooftop assassin was taking careful aim at its target; patiently waiting for the right moment to pull the trigger on the silenced high-powered rifle.

Several speeches spoken until it was Hawk's turn to speak.

As he stood before the crowd, loud cheers echoed through the park. Raising a hand to silence the excited crowd, no one knew a rifle had gone off. All the people noticed was Hawk trying to quiet down the crowd to speak and then the next moment he froze in place. Blood began coming out of the middle of his forehead, just before his eyes rolled up into his head and his body fell backwards.

Edwards Brothers Malloy
Oxnard, CA  USA
April 23, 2014